All He Could Se...
Guest Was...

It was all he needed to... been using common sense, travelling unknowingly into a blizzard, but she was definitely an eyeful. Not that short, green-eyed redheads were his usual type. He preferred cool blondes with long legs .

But he'd been hard-pressed to remember he was a gentleman and not sneak a peak while she was changing earlier. He was a gentleman, but he was only human. And standing there with his back to an attractive woman while listening to the seductive sound of zippers and shifting clothing had put his chivalry to the ultimate test.

And he didn't realize just how sexy his oversize clothes could look on a woman. A woman who was sleeping in his bed...

Dear Reader

As November brings cold days and dark nights, what better way to spend your time than curled up indoors reading our fantastic Desire™ line-up!

Firstly, welcome back top author Ann Major who brings us our **Man of the Month**, sizzlingly sexy film star, Joey Fasano. And then meet two irresistible cop heroes. Andy Gautier is called upon to investigate a woman's mysterious memory loss in *Her Holiday Secret* by Jennifer Greene. And Marie Ferrarella brings us the latest instalment in her Cutler family saga where Sheriff Quint Cutler puts his future wife in jail!

Everybody's looking for a missing pregnant woman in our **Follow That Baby** cross-line mini-series which continues this month with *The Daddy and the Baby Doctor*. Don't miss the next two instalments in December and January, also in Desire, and then the exciting conclusion in February in the Sensation™ series!

Finally, to round off this month's line-up, enjoy a delightful baby story from Christy Lockhart and envy Pamela Macaluso's lucky heroine who's sheltered from a storm by a handsome stranger.

Happy reading!

The Editors

The Cowboy Who Came in From the Cold

PAMELA MACALUSO

SILHOUETTE
DESIRE

*First published in Great Britain 1999
Silhouette Books, Eton House, 18-24 Paradise Road,
Richmond, Surrey TW9 1SR*

© Pamela Macaluso 1998

ISBN 0 373 76152 X

22-9911

*Printed and bound in Spain
by Litografia Rosés S.A., Barcelona*

PAMELA MACALUSO

wanted to be a writer from the moment she realized people actually wrote the wonderful stories that were read to her. Since she is extremely curious and has an overactive imagination, writing is the perfect career for her.

While she loves movies, Pamela would choose a good book over any other form of entertainment.

Other novels by Pamela Macaluso

For Karen Taylor Richman, my editor.

Many thanks for all your insight
and guidance on this book.

And for Pammy, whose quiet intelligence and gentle
spirit have ultimately prevailed over those who doubted,
providing inspiration through the realization of a dream.

One

"You might as well get into the truck, lady. I'm not leaving you here. A snow flurry is one thing, but a blizzard is something completely different."

Patrice Caldwell looked from her sports car resting in the shallow ditch to the tall stranger. He was bundled up from the cold. All she could see of his face was the vague shape of his eyes in the shadow of his Stetson. For all she knew he could be a crazed ax murderer.

She glanced at his truck. No ax, but there was a rifle in the back window. Lack of sleep, the long hours of driving and the turmoil that had sent her on this mad dash from Phoenix, Arizona, to somewhere in Montana weighed heavily on her.

She spoke her thoughts without considering how they would sound. "Freezing would be less painful than bleeding to death from a gunshot wound."

The stranger shook his head and said something she couldn't quite make out because of the muffling layers of scarf covering his face. Before she could ask him to repeat what he'd said, he stepped forward and scooped her into his arms.

Patrice had been swept off her feet figuratively before, but this was the first time it had happened literally. It was unsettling to say the least. Even through layers of clothing, she could tell this guy had a rock-hard body. Struggling to get away *wasn't* an option. In size and muscle power he held all the cards. She would have to be sure any battle between them was a battle of wits.

Right, Patrice, like your wits are in any kind of competent shape after a day and a half with little sleep and over twenty-four hours on the road.

He carried her to the truck. When he opened the door, the heated air hit her face in a blast of warmth. He set her in the driver's seat because that was closest to where they'd stood. For an instant she considered throwing the engine in gear and driving away, but he was right behind her. Because of his height, the bench seat was back far enough that it was easy for her to scoot across to the other side—all the way to the passenger door.

The stranger started the truck moving as soon as he got in and closed the door.

Patrice looked back at her car. She hated to abandon it this way. They'd come so far together in the past twenty-four hours that a special bond now linked them. It had never been more than a way to get to and from work, until her whole life had come crashing down around her, and then it had become her means of escape. Now she was saying "Thank you" by abandoning it.

Her thoughts snapped to reality when she remembered the personal items she'd brought on the trip with her. "Wait! My luggage!" How could she have forgotten?

The stranger continued to accelerate. "It won't go anywhere."

The suitcase was in the trunk. "My briefcase and laptop are in the back seat, and my cellular phone is on the front seat, and I didn't lock the door."

He peeled the scarf off the lower half of his face, tucking it around his neck. It didn't give her any better view of her rescuer, since he had a dark beard covering his chin and jaw, and a mustache that hid his top lip. All that was new to the picture was his nose and full bottom lip. But it was enough for her to know this man was a looker—in that sexy rugged mountain man way.

Now that his eyes weren't squinting to protect them from the frigid wind, she could see them better. They were an incredible shade of blue...and framed by thick dark lashes.

He had great eyes, seductive eyes, except at the moment, the message they were sending was one of annoyance, not enticement. "Lady, your stuff will be safe. No one is dumb enough to be out in this weather."

"Meaning *no one else* is dumb enough to be out in this weather."

He glanced her way. No words were necessary; the glance spoke volumes.

Did he have any idea how stop-in-your-tracks good-looking he was?

What was she thinking? A stranger picks her up along the side of the road and all she can think about is how attractive he is? Maybe her brain had frostbite.

Technically he was a stranger to her, but an expected stranger, and one she was relieved to see. She'd spoken to the sheriff of Clancy, Montana, and he'd said he would send someone with a tow truck to help her.

Suddenly she realized she wasn't sitting in a tow truck. "Sheriff Jackson said he was calling someone with a tow truck," she said nervously, slightly suspicious of her rescuer.

"I have one. But at the moment, it's on the far side of the ranch. Besides, we never would have made it in time."

"In time for what?"

"In time to be back safely before the storm gets going."

"You're really expecting a blizzard?"

He took a deep breath and let it out. Even with the heater on the highest setting, a white puff of condensation accompanied it. "Surely those fancy city wheels of yours must have a radio. Haven't you been listening to it?"

She'd been listening to CDs—soft, soothing music, in an attempt to counter the turmoil in her mind and spirit.

"Yes, the car has a radio, but I hadn't been listening to it."

He shook his head. "Didn't you notice the clouds gathering?"

Earlier, all her attention had been on the road. Two lanes, wet where the snow hit and melted.

Knowing where the conversation was heading, she didn't answer him. After the past thirty-six hours, the last thing she needed was some modern-day Jeremiah Johnson lecturing her about being on the road without keeping track of the weather.

She settled into her seat, rubbing her gloved hands together. Thank heaven she'd bought the gloves, hat, scarf and snow boots the last time she'd stopped for gas. She was cold enough with them. Being without would have been unthinkable. A heavier jacket would have helped, too. Something like the sheepskin-lined coat the man beside her was wearing.

The stranger slowed the truck, looking to the left. A minute later, he turned, steering between two metal stakes. There was a shallow buildup of snow on what seemed more like a trail leading into the forest than a road. He put the truck into four-wheel drive.

Patrice looked around trying to memorize the surroundings—just in case. But she couldn't make out any discernible landmarks. There were lots of trees and a number of rocks, all dusted with white snow. None were distinctive enough to make a good marker. Metal stakes were posted at regular intervals, marking the trail, but she had no idea how many similar trails were in the area. Would she be able to find her way back alone and on foot if she had to make a run for it?

Part of her was nervous and on guard, while the other part urged her to give the guy the benefit of the doubt, trusting that he really was there to help, not indulge in nefarious deeds. Her budding trust was shaken when the trail narrowed even more, curved and started upward.

"We're going higher? Shouldn't we be heading down the mountain?"

"The nearest shelter is this way."

Shelter? How did he define shelter?

The flakes were falling faster, whirling around

before splatting against the windshield, and there were more of them joining in the dance as time passed. A shiver of unease passed through her as she finally admitted to herself that he might be right about the blizzard after all.

They drove another five minutes or so, then the road widened into a clearing. In the middle of it was a snow-covered log cabin. Patrice would have appreciated it more as a photo on a Christmas card than up close and personal as she sat shivering in a pickup truck.

The stranger pulled around to the side of the cabin, parked beside a lean-to and turned off the engine. Without the rumbling and the whooshing of the heater, the wail of the wind echoed outside the truck's cab. Her mysterious rescuer reached across her and took a cellular phone out of the glove compartment. Tucking the phone into his pocket, he opened the driver's side door, slid out, then grabbed the rifle.

Patrice couldn't stop her quick intake of breath. "Do you have to bring that? I mean, can't you leave it in the truck?"

"Most bears are hibernating this time of year, so if one shows up, it's liable to be extra cranky." He closed the driver's door and headed for the cabin.

Bears?

Patrice looked in all directions before hopping out of the truck and quickly following him to the narrow porch. A wooden sign hung over the door. Burned into it was the letter G nestled inside a larger letter C, and next to that, the number five.

Inside, the cabin looked larger than it did from the outside, but it was still a long way from what anyone would call spacious. And it was dark. Light struggled through the shuttered windows and only the open doorway made a dent in the darkness.

The man took off his gloves and lit the two kerosene lanterns sitting on the wooden table. He left one on the table and set the other on top of the dresser sitting next to a set of bunk beds. The only other furniture in the room was two benches along either side of the table and a small couch.

"Close the door."

She did as he asked. Leaning against the heavy wooden barrier, ready to make a run for it if needed, she watched him light fires in the stone fireplace and the woodstove. When she noticed he'd left the rifle on a rack beside the door, she felt more at ease.

He took the phone from his pocket and dialed. "Mack? It's Stone. I've got her." He tipped his Stetson back a bit. A lock of hair fell over his forehead. It was a shade darker than his beard. "Yeah, we made it safely to number five. Let Jackson know, will you? I'll call again in a few days." He paused. "Right. Talk to you later."

Stone, his name was Stone. It suited him—rugged and hard. "Is Stone your first or last name?"

"First."

Patrice inched her way into the room, leaving her safe haven by the door. Stepping closer toward him, she slipped off her right glove and reached out her hand. "I'm Patrice Caldwell. It's nice to meet you, Stone."

He looked at her hand, then slowly reached out and took it in his. She was immediately struck by how much larger his hand was and how much warmer. His grip was firm, but in a comforting way, not threatening.

He let go of her hand. "You'd better get your glove back on, ma'am. Your hands are colder than ice cubes." He turned and headed for a pantry cupboard across the room. "I'll make some coffee."

After Stone had gathered what he needed and walked to the stove, Patrice investigated the cupboard. There was an inventory posted on the inside of the door and labels on the shelves identifying where everything belonged. And to think her friends had teased her about being overly organized.

"Have you lived here long?"

He let out a short, dry laugh. "I don't live here. This is a line shack. Someplace for the ranch hands to stay when they're out riding fence or working the herd and it gets too late to go back to the ranch for the night. Or someplace to hole up if the weather turns nasty...like today."

"Oh." She closed the cupboard. "Are you a cowboy?"

There were ranches and cowboys in Arizona, but Patrice had never actually met one before. For her, cowboys were the larger-than-life heroes that she'd watched, along with her father, during the Wild West movie marathons on TV.

"I'm a cowboy."

"Do you like your job?"

He shrugged. "I guess. I've never given it much thought." He turned. "The coffee will be ready in a bit. Meantime, let's see about getting you some warmer clothes." He walked to the dresser. "They're on the large side, but they're the smallest we've got."

The thermal underwear, blue jeans and flannel shirt he brought her would be much warmer than the linen pantsuit she was wearing.

"Thanks."

"I'll get a jacket for you to wear until it warms up in here."

He rifled through a second cupboard near the first one. Inside she could see sleeping bags, pillows, stacks of blankets and towels, as well as a supply of jackets, hats and gloves.

Patrice looked around the small cabin. The only door was the one they'd come in. "Um, is there somewhere I can change?"

"What you see is what you get."

A strong gust of wind rattled the shutters. Dare she suggest he wait outside?

"You'll keep your back turned, won't you?"

"Of course."

He brought her the jacket then stood in front of the fireplace to give her some privacy.

"I'm going to change now, if that's okay."

"Yes, ma'am. Let me know when you're finished."

She walked to the bunk beds, setting the clothes on the top mattress. Turning her back to him, she shrugged out of her clothes and put on the others. Roomy was an understatement, but already she could feel the extra warmth and was grateful.

She turned toward the fireplace and her breath caught in her throat. He still had his back to her, that wasn't the problem. What disturbed her was the vision he created. Like something out of a fantasy. He had one arm raised and leaning against the mantel, the other rested at his side and held his hat. The red-orange tinged light from the fire flickered as it cast its glow over him. His jacket was long, hiding his backside, but making his denim-clad legs look that much longer, and powerful.

She reached her hand to her mouth to stop the whistle of appreciation that threatened to escape and got a face full of flannel.

A quick inspection of her attire confirmed what she already suspected. He might look like a fantasy come to life, but she looked like a five-year-old playing dress up.

Laughing, she started to roll up the sleeves. "You can turn around now. I'm decent."

After the sleeves, she tackled the pant legs. She looked up and stopped laughing. He was watching her. While she couldn't interpret his expression, the intensity of his gaze had her wondering if she'd forgotten some article of clothing.

"There's rope in the cupboard you can use as a belt." His voice had an extra huskiness to it.

"All right." Patrice easily found the rope. Fortunately there were already some pieces cut, and one was the exact size she needed.

When she turned, Stone was still standing in front of the fire, looking too at home, too handsome and *way* too sexy.

He took a step forward. "The coffee should be just about ready."

"Coffee." She repeated the word, but it had no meaning at first. Only as he poured the dark brew into two speckled blue enamel mugs did the fog in her mind clear.

"How do you take it?"

"Usually with a little milk."

"Is powdered creamer all right?"

She nodded. She wasn't in a position to be picky.

They sat on opposite sides of the table on the end farthest from the lantern.

Patrice sipped her coffee, then wrapped her hands around the warm mug.

An unsettling thought weaseled its way into her mind. "There's only one room here."

"Like I said, what you see is what you get. If you're worried about sleeping arrangements, don't be. I'll stay in my own bunk, and I don't snore."

Good grief! She hadn't even gotten around to worrying about sleeping arrangements. And she needed to. Once asleep, she would be absolutely, positively at his mercy!

Only first things first. "What I was wondering about was, um, the facilities? The bathroom?"

"The outhouse."

"Right."

"It's out back."

"It's snowing out there."

He took a drink from his mug before answering. "I know. That's why we're here."

"But the bathroom is out back?"

"Yes, ma'am."

"Who designed this place?"

"It's intended for occasional use only, and it wouldn't be cost-effective to install modern plumbing."

"What about some not-so-modern plumbing?"

He smiled, the first real smile she'd seen on him. She felt it all the way to her toes. He shook his head.

Patrice sighed. "Not cost-effective?" She tilted her head, looking at him. Cost-effective wasn't typical cowboy lingo. Maybe he was foreman or ranch manager. "Getting eaten by a bear can't be cost-effective, either."

There was that smile again. She caught a glimpse of it before he hid it by drinking his coffee.

She took a sip from her mug. Already the contents were starting to cool.

"An angry deer can be dangerous, too," he said.

Terrific! Bears and her too-sexy rescuer weren't perilous enough.

She remembered the large deer she'd swerved to avoid hitting before ending up in the ditch. "Are all the deer around here extra large?"

"There are some good-size animals in the area. What do you consider extra large?"

"The size of a small horse."

He raised one brow in question. "You saw a deer the size of a small horse?" he asked disbelievingly.

"It was crossing the road."

"It was probably an elk," he corrected.

"An elk? Are they any friendlier than deer or the insomniac bears?"

He chuckled. "'Fraid not."

"It figures. I don't think I'm cut out for this wilderness thing," she confessed.

"I could have told you that," he said honestly.

She set her mug down. "How can you say that? You don't even know me."

"I don't have to. If you were used to the wilderness, you wouldn't be driving a convertible through the mountains of Montana with a storm coming."

"The top was on."

He shrugged. She waited for him to launch into the lecture she'd expected earlier. Instead he asked if she wanted more coffee.

"No, thanks." She stood. "I'm going to take a short walk."

"Out back?"

She nodded.

"Let me make sure nothing has decided to nest out there since the last time the place was used."

Nesting things? She didn't even want to know what the possibilities were. "Be my guest."

Once Stone was back, Patrice headed out. It was still light outside, but it was clear nightfall was on the way. The amount of snow falling had increased, too, but not enough to block visibility of her destination.

She was almost back to the cabin when Stone came around the corner holding a rope. A flutter of fear settled in her stomach. "I was just on my way back." She tried to sound casual while glancing around for something to pick up and use as a club.

"I'm going to string up a line between the end

of the cabin and the outhouse, in case you need to get out there after dark or in a whiteout.''

''Oh…thank you.'' She felt silly for letting her wild imagination get to her.

''Don't mention it, ma'am.'' He tipped his hat, then headed toward the corner of the cabin.

Patrice went back inside. She slipped off her gloves and stood in front of the fireplace, holding her hands toward the flames.

When she heard the sound of Stone's boots stomping on the porch, she went back to full alert.

''Let me add a few more logs there,'' he said.

Patrice moved. Standing to the side, she watched him. He looked right at home, completely in his element.

A yawn escaped her. ''Pardon me.''

He glanced over his shoulder. ''You've had a rough day, runnin' off the road and all. Maybe you should turn in.''

Okay, Patrice, now's the time to worry about the sleeping arrangements.

Two

Stone pulled several sleeping bags and pillows out of the cupboard. He set one pair on the top bunk, the other on the bottom.

"I suggest you sleep on top."

Patrice knew he meant the top bunk, but his words created a vivid image in her mind. An image that involved her being on top, not of the bunk and not for sleeping. "Warm air rises. I know, I took physics," she said, trying to ease the awkward moment.

"I didn't take physics, but I've slept in both of these bunks, and you'll be warmer in the top one."

She untied the sleeping bag and unrolled it across

the mattress, conscious of his gaze on her. Fluffing the pillow, she tried to act as nonchalant about the whole situation as he did. No reason for him to know the thought of spending the night here alone with him unnerved her.

He continued, "The end of the bed is a ladder."

"I noticed." She was surprised by the snap in her voice. It wasn't like her, but then the way he was explaining things—how to get into a bunk bed—made it seem as though he thought she was a complete idiot.

"Look, I know I made a mistake driving up here without checking the weather, but I'm perfectly capable of putting myself to bed for the night."

His gaze narrowed, and she expected him to snap back. Instead he nodded toward the bunk. "Get some sleep."

Patrice climbed onto the mattress, slipped into the sleeping bag and rested her head on the pillow. She watched Stone adding wood to the stove. When he finished, he poured himself another mug of coffee and walked across the room to the fireplace.

Walked didn't quite describe his movements, she decided. Ambled came closer, since his motions were easy, casual and relaxed. She was struck again by how handsome he was and how he looked so natural in the surroundings. It felt as if she were watching a cowboy movie from front row center.

Despite her earlier fears about her vulnerability

while asleep, the warmth of the sleeping bag and the softness of the pillow were seducing her senses toward sleep.

Just before she drifted off, she remembered Stone's words, "I'll stay in my own bunk, and I don't snore."

How did he know he didn't snore?

Stone angled the sofa closer to the fire before he stretched out on it. The small love seat wasn't nearly long enough for him to get too comfortable.

He had to make do while a much larger couch and oversize recliner sat empty at the house. Then again his Labrador retriever, Elwood, was probably taking advantage of his absence to make himself at home.

He glanced toward the bunk beds. The sides of the room were shadowed so that about all he could see of his unexpected guest was a silhouette.

It was all he needed to see. She might not have much common sense, traveling unknowingly into a blizzard, but she was definitely an eyeful. Not that short, sassy, green-eyed redheads were his usual type. He preferred cool blondes with long legs.

He'd been hard-pressed to remember he was a gentleman and not sneak a peek while she was changing earlier. He was a gentleman, but he was only human. And standing there with his back to an attractive woman while listening to the sound of zippers and shifting material had put his chivalry to the ultimate test.

Patrice Caldwell. The woman's name suited her, as did her tailored clothing and flashy red car. She was a city slicker through and through, but he had to admit the oversize cowboy duds he'd given her to wear looked kind of cute. That had been a surprise, turning around to find the icy, serious Patrice laughing and smiling as she rolled up the sleeves of the borrowed shirt.

He couldn't help fantasizing about getting her back out of those warm clothes and into a sleeping bag with him....

Especially when the feel of carrying her to the truck was fresh in his memory. She was petite, but curvy in all the right places, and, Lord help him, he liked a woman to have curves. Yep, she was a pleasing armful and eyeful, all right.

He felt a smile tug at the corners of his mouth as he thought about her reaction when he'd told her about the outhouse. And her comment about the deer and insomniac bears!

For a moment he almost felt sorry for her, but then he reminded himself, Patrice was the reason he was stuck here on a too-small couch with a quickly cooling cup of coffee, instead of watching a football game from the recliner in his den.

At least he didn't have to worry about things at the ranch. His foreman, Mack, was top-notch and would take care of business. His housekeeper, Virginia, would hold down the homefront.

The bad part about being stuck here was figuring out how to keep occupied. If he didn't stay busy, he would go nuts. There was a small assortment of books, magazines and games in each of the line shacks, but the prospect didn't excite him at the moment...not nearly as much as his unexpected roommate did.

The shutters rattled with the increasing wind gusts. His wife used to love listening to the wind late at night. Especially when it would hit the eaves at the right angle to make a whistling sound.

No way, buddy, don't start thinking about Valerie.

A log shifted in the fireplace, sending up a shower of sparks. He took a deep breath and let it out slowly. The cabin was starting to warm up. He would keep the fires going full force for the next few hours then catch some sleep.

He glanced toward the bunk again. Patrice hadn't moved. She was probably fast asleep by now. This was going to be some night. A true test of his self-control. Because he'd never shared a bunk bed with a woman before...well, never in separate bunks.

Patrice's body was so tired it ached. Her mind was frazzled and tired, too, but it didn't want to stop racing.

This was the second time she'd awoken. The first time had been when Stone had been adding logs to the fire. From the noise below, and since the lamps were off, she assumed this time what had disturbed her was his calling it a night.

Her heartbeat raced. No need to panic, he's in his own bunk, and he said he would stay there. From the sound of the wind outside, she had no choice but to trust that she was safe with him.

And...he won't snore. Once again she wondered how he knew. Was there someone he slept with on a regular basis waiting for him at home? A wife? Live-in girlfriend? Somebody who might not like the idea of his spending the night in a cabin with another woman?

What difference did it make? Tomorrow they would be out of here, and she probably wouldn't ever see him again.

A popping noise came from the fireplace and she jumped. There was movement and more rustling from below, as though Stone were settling more deeply into his sleeping bag. Patrice fought back a nervous giggle as she realized this was the closest she'd ever come to sleeping with a man. There was a mattress and several feet of air between them, but they were still sleeping together.

This was definitely *not* how she'd pictured her first night with a man.

Then again this was not the man she'd pictured

herself with. Though she had to admit he was attractive. His eyes were incredible. How many women had he seduced with just a look?

What would it feel like to have him look at me that way?

Finally she felt the brush of sleep flirting with her once again. Pondering the question, she drifted off.

The smell of freshly brewing coffee woke her in the morning. Patrice opened her eyes slowly. The lamps were lit, and the small crack of dim light between the shutters announced that it was some time after sunrise. Stone was sitting at the table, a book open in front of him. The wind still howled past the cabin.

She started to move, but every muscle in her body protested. Biting her bottom lip to keep from groaning, she wriggled out of the sleeping bag and slowly sat up. "Good morning."

He nodded in her direction. "Mornin'."

It sure didn't sound good from the wind outside. "Is the blizzard still going strong?"

"Yep, from what I heard yesterday, it should let up day after tomorrow."

Patrice was sure she'd heard him incorrectly. "Day after tomorrow?"

"Yes, ma'am."

"You mean we can't leave here until the day

after tomorrow?'' What on earth would they do stuck in this cabin until then?

"We can't leave until some of the snow melts."

She didn't like the sound of this. "When the snow melts?"

"We're low enough that when the Chinook comes, enough of it will melt for us to drive out."

"I don't mean to play twenty questions, but what is the Chinook? And when is it coming?" she asked sincerely.

"A Chinook is a warm wind. And it should be here in a week, or so."

When he'd told whomever he'd talked to on the phone that he'd call again in a few days, she never dreamed he meant that he'd be placing the call from here. "A week? Or so?"

"Hey, this is no picnic for me, either."

His words hit her like a blast of cold air, making her feel ungrateful and selfish. If the storm wouldn't let up until the day after tomorrow, he'd probably saved her life by getting her out of and away from her stuck car. "I appreciate your coming to my rescue. I guess I should have said thank you yesterday. Better late than never?"

"You're welcome, Patrice." He stood. "Oatmeal for breakfast?"

She wrinkled her nose.

A half smile tugged at his mouth. "Better get used to the idea. There's not a lot of variety. Most stays here are only a few days at a time. So while we won't starve, the menu will be limited, and it's not going to be gourmet fare.''

"Like you said, this isn't a picnic. Is there anything I can do to help?" She headed for the end of the bed, wincing when her foot hit the first rung.

"A little sore this morning?"

"A *lot* sore." She finished her climb down and rolled her shoulders back and forward, trying to loosen up some of the stiffness. "I don't understand it, the bed felt comfortable enough when I crawled in it last night."

"The stiffening is most likely from the accident yesterday.''

He was probably right. That whole problem of automatically tensing your muscles before impact, the reason why sleeping passengers and drivers under the influence often escaped serious injury.

"With everything else, I'd forgotten about that.'' The threat of wild animals and spending her first night with a man—a gorgeous one at that—had brushed the accident right out of her mind. Both the accident and the events leading up to it.

"There are painkillers and ointment in the first-aid kit.''

Patrice easily found aspirin in the well-organized cupboard. She also glanced through the packaged and canned food. The supply was plentiful, but there wasn't much variety. Stone was right, they wouldn't starve. And since most everything was heat-and-serve or add-hot-water, meal preparation was going to be a snap.

They worked side by side getting breakfast ready and cleaning up. Afterward, Stone went outside to bring in more wood and gather buckets of snow so they wouldn't use up their bottled water for washing and dishes.

When she could put it off no longer, Patrice made the trip to the outhouse. The brutal wind cut through all the layers of her clothing. It was amazing how much snow had fallen during the night, and it was still coming down.

Once back inside the cabin, she stood in front of the fire.

"I thought it was cold in here until I went out," she said, being truthful.

"It *is* cold in here. It's just colder out there."

"I guess. *Brrr,* is an understatement."

She turned her back to the fire so that she could defrost evenly. Stone was sitting on one end of the couch. The book he'd been reading sat open in his lap.

There was an awkward silence. She laughed, nervously. "Well, we've introduced ourselves and discussed the weather. Now what?"

"There are some books and things in the cupboard," he directed.

"More than a week's worth?"

"Read slowly," he said sarcastically.

Patrice sighed. "I guess electricity and a computer wouldn't be cost-effective out here, either."

"Nope. And if we had electricity, I'd put in a TV and VCR before a computer. More people could use it at the same time." He closed his book and set it next to him on the couch.

"I never would have expected cost-effectiveness to be such a concern for a cowboy."

"Ranching is a business."

"I guess I never stopped to think about it. I hear the word cowboy and automatically think about men in boots and hats riding horses and driving pickup trucks."

He smiled one of his killer smiles. "That's the fun part, but there's a whole lot more to ranching than that."

"And I'm keeping you from work, aren't I? I'm sorry." An awful thought crossed her mind. "You won't lose your job because you're stuck here, will you? If you need me to explain things to your boss—"

"I *am* the boss. My job's not in any danger as long as beef prices stay up and we don't lose too many cattle over the winter."

"That's a relief. I feel bad enough about stranding us. If I'd jeopardized your job on top of that, it would be even worse." She wondered about the effect on his private life, but wasn't about to ask.

Was she afraid to hear that he had a wife and half a dozen kids waiting for him?

She glanced at his left hand. He wasn't wearing a ring, although that wasn't necessarily conclusive with such a rugged career.

But if he did have a wife, wouldn't he have called home? Of course he might have done so while she was in the outhouse. Besides, it shouldn't matter. The last thing she needed right now was another man in her life.

"So, what brings you to Montana?" he asked.

"My grandmother lives in Clancy."

"Does she know you've been delayed? Would you like to call her?"

"Actually she doesn't know I'm coming. I was planning to surprise her." She sighed. "I guess I should have called first. She would have warned me about the storm."

But Grandma would have heard the hurt and despair in her voice, and she would have ended up pouring out her troubles over the phone. She wanted to do it in person, where Grandma was close enough to offer the comfort of hugs, a cup of tea and warm cinnamon rolls.

"How're the sore muscles?" Stone asked.

"Better for the most part. Except my right leg. Probably from slamming so hard on the brake pedal."

"I can massage some of the knots out of it, if you'd like."

The last time a guy had worked knots out of her muscles it had ended up costing her her business and close to every dollar she owned. "No, thanks. The aspirin will be kicking in soon."

"Well, the offer stands, and I'm not trying to make a pass at you."

The thought hadn't even occurred to her. Maybe it should have. Was that his game, lulling her into complacency and then attacking?

Now don't start that again, Patrice. He rescued you and has been a perfect gentleman.

Besides, with his looks, he probably has a steady woman in his life, or a string of women.

"I didn't think you were trying to make a pass."

Something flashed in his eyes. "And if I had been?"

She wasn't sure if the sparkle in his eyes was laughter or something else entirely. Was he teasing or trying to gage her reaction to see if she might be receptive to a sexual advance? "But you weren't."

"You can use your imagination."

No, that wasn't a good idea. Her imagination could get her into a lot of trouble in this situation…especially since during the night she'd let it ponder the question of what it would feel like to have him turn a seductive gaze her way.

She wasn't about to tell him that in the scenarios she'd envisioned, she had returned his advances with enthusiasm—melting into his arms, returning his kisses. And even worse was the possibility that if he were to make a real pass, she might be unable to stop herself from doing just that.

No one who knew her would believe her capable of such a wildly spontaneous action, but then they hadn't laid eyes on Stone, or had him settle his baby blues on them.

Amazing how in less than twenty-four hours she'd grown less suspicious of him and more fascinated by his rugged masculinity. Amazing...since she'd always preferred the sophisticated business-suit type.

And look where that got you!

All the long hours and hard work she'd put into building her bookkeeping service and what did she have to show for it? An engagement ring, which had turned out to be a cubic zirconium, and her car, which was stuck in a ditch in the middle of a blizzard.

She hoped it would be all right, since she'd been planning on trading it in when she got home. She needed the cash to hold her until she found a job.

If her credibility wasn't totally shot in the Phoenix area...

"Are you going to answer my question?"

"I really think it's for the best if I don't," she admitted.

He shrugged. "Here's an easier one. Are you planning to be at your grandmother's long?"

"I'd thought about a week."

"Will you be able to get an extension on your vacation time?"

"I'm, uh, between jobs at the moment."

"A recent development?"

"Very recent." She hadn't been completely successful at keeping the catch out of her voice. "I guess I'll check out the selection of books."

She didn't want to discuss her lack of a job, knowing that when she did the tears would come. She'd waited this long to share the tale and seek comfort in Grandma's arms, she could wait another week or so.

Stone might offer the comfort of his arms...but could any red-blooded female be in them and only think of comfort?

Three

————

"Would we really lose that much heat if we opened the shutters?" Patrice asked late in the afternoon when she was about to go stir-crazy.

"It would get draftier."

It was already drafty. "I'd just like to see some of the daylight."

"Feeling closed in?"

She nodded.

Stone put on his jacket, scarf, hat and gloves. Once outside, he opened the shutters on the two windows on the front side of the cabin.

Patrice went over to look out. It was cloudy and overcast, but the sight of the meadow and what she could see of the trees through the snow was a nice break from the four walls of the cabin. At times she could see snowflakes falling to the ground, other times it seemed they were sailing horizontally across the sky.

Viewed through the intricate frost patterns on the window, everything was beautiful and picture-perfect.

For the first time since she'd discovered her ex-fiancé's betrayal, a sense of peace settled over her. Yes, her life was a mess, but her life couldn't reach her right now. The snow seemed like a protector. Instead of a barrier keeping her in, it was a shelter keeping the world out. She took a deep breath, letting it out slowly.

The prospect of being able to lick her wounds in peace sounded appealing. So far she'd focused on the financial end, but knew she couldn't keep avoiding the most hurtful aspects of things—the emotional betrayal. Mountains of hurt and anger were building inside her...not just because he'd been enough of a creep to rob her blind, but because she'd been foolish enough to fall for him.

Stone passed in front of the window, carrying an armful of logs. She went to the door to let him in.

"Thanks," he said, stomping the snow off his boots and returning to the warmth inside.

Patrice closed the door and took her place next to the window, letting the beauty entrance and soothe her once more. The sound of Stone stacking the wood became part of the assuagement.

"Do you get much snow in your part of Arizona?" He was now standing behind her.

She glanced over her shoulder at him. "How do you know I'm from Arizona?"

"Your license plate."

"I'm from Phoenix. Snow is rare." She looked back out the window. "It really is beautiful up here."

"I've always thought so."

"Do you get snowed in often?" she asked.

"Not for long, the main part of the ranch is at a lower elevation, and we have a snowplow."

"Have you been stranded up here before?"

"I was up here last winter by myself for a week."

"You were stuck here *alone?*"

"Yes."

"Sounds scary. I'm glad you're here with me." She glanced over her shoulder. He'd moved a few steps closer.

His gaze dropped briefly to her lips then returned to her eyes. "Are you?"

Her heartbeat seemed to trip over itself, then picked up speed. If she turned and took a step, she could be in his arms.

His gaze found her mouth again, and she almost gave in to the temptation.

The crackle of a log in the fireplace stopped her in time. "Yes, I wouldn't want to be here alone."

A half smile tugged at the corners of his mouth. "Darlin', if you had any idea what's been going through my mind the last few minutes, you'd wish me out of here in a heartbeat."

Quickly she turned back to the window. She thought about the way he'd looked at her mouth. Had he been thinking about kissing her, even as she'd been dreaming and pondering what it would feel like to have him turn the force of his charms her way?

Before she could change her mind, she turned fully around to face him. "Why do you say that?"

She thought he wasn't going to answer, but then he said, "I've been wondering most of the day what it would feel like to kiss you, and the last few minutes I've been giving serious consideration to finding out."

She caught her bottom lip between her teeth and nibbled on it. What *would* it feel like to kiss him?

"I've never been kissed by a man with a beard." She had no idea why that fact had tumbled out of her mouth...maybe because it was harmless compared to the other thoughts she was having.

How can you want him to kiss you when you've known him less than a day?

He rubbed his fingers along his jawline. "I usually grow a beard in the winter. It helps keep my face warm." He took half a step toward her. "It's not as rough or scratchy as it looks." He reached out and took her hand, bringing it to rest against his cheek.

Her breath caught in her throat. He was right, it wasn't as rough as it looked. She could imagine the feel of it brushing against her cheeks...across the swell of her breasts...on the sensitive skin of her inner thigh....

There was a hint of warmth coming from his skin beneath. Her fingertips tingled, and she fought back the urge to run her thumb over the fullness of his bottom lip.

She looked into his eyes. They had darkened to a deeper, more striking blue. It would be too easy to let herself fall into them. She forced herself to blink, to break the spell.

"Why?" she asked.

"Why isn't it as scratchy as it looks?"

"Why do you want to kiss me?"

"Why do you want me to?"

She pulled her hand from his face and moved away until she felt the cabin wall against her back. "I didn't say that I wanted you to kiss me."

He smiled. "You didn't have to say the words, it was written all over your face."

It crossed her mind to lie, but she told the truth. "I honestly don't know why."

He moved to the couch. "Is there a significant other waiting for you back in Arizona?"

She shook her head. "I was engaged, but that ended the same time I lost my job."

"Were the two related?"

"Yes, but I'd rather not talk about it."

He shrugged. "All right."

"Is there a significant other waiting for you back at the ranch?"

A troubled look passed over his features. "No. I'm a widower."

"I'm sorry."

"It's been two years."

The obvious questions crossed her mind: How had he lost his wife, how long had they been married? But she didn't want to pry. Besides, what mattered most was that he was currently unattached, and she was surprisingly glad.

She realized he hadn't answered her question about why he'd wanted to kiss her. And apparently he'd changed his mind, since he stood so far away....

He rubbed his hand across his beard where she had so recently touched. "We could play some cards. There's a deck in the cupboard. Unless you'd like to get back to your book?"

"Let's try cards for a while. Although I'm afraid I don't know many card games."

They ended up pulling the cribbage board out of

the game box. Patrice had never played, so Stone taught her. He was a thorough and patient teacher. She couldn't stop from speculating whether he'd be a thorough and patient lover, as well.

Stone shuffled the cards. "Clancy is a fairly small town. What's your grandmother's name? I may know her."

"Dorothy Winston."

"Dorothy Winston? The Mrs. Winston that teaches at Clancy High?"

"She used to."

"She taught one of my senior year classes."

Patrice tried to picture a younger high-school-age Stone. She would bet money he'd been breaking hearts even then.

"I always wished I could be in a class of hers. Was she a good teacher?"

"The best. One of the only English classes I enjoyed in school." A wistful smile curved his lips. "I met Val in Mrs. Winston's English class."

Patrice made a mental note to ask her grandmother about Val and Stone. She wasn't sure what good knowing about the other woman would do, other than give her an idea of the kind of woman Stone was attracted to. A topic she was better off *not* exploring.

Before she knew it, the light coming in through the windows was starting to fade.

"I'd better make a trip out back before it gets dark," she said.

"Good idea."

Once the necessities and dinner were taken care of, Stone went out and closed the shutters for the night. "We'll open them again during the day tomorrow."

They settled in on opposite sides of the couch with their books.

"I keep forgetting to ask, what do the C and G over the door stand for?" Patrice said.

"That's our brand. Baron Garrett Cattle Company."

"Baron Garrett as in Baron and Garrett, or titled aristocracy?"

"The baron claimed to be titled. But he arrived here in the 1890s. Back then, as slow as news traveled, he could have claimed to be the king of England himself and no one would have been able to prove otherwise. There's a portrait of him at the ranch. Tall, blond, very aristocratic looking."

"Is there any way to find out whether he was really a baron?"

"I'm sure there is. Val talked about researching and finding out the truth, but she didn't get around to it."

"Val was your wife?"

"Yes. I told her she only wanted to know because she wanted to say she was a baroness."

"You're related to the baron?"

"He was my great-great-grandfather."

He hadn't told her his full name yesterday. Stone Garrett. It sounded like a good name for a cowboy, and it suited him.

"Are you the eldest son of an eldest son?"

"The only son of an only son."

"So you might be a baron? Should I call you my Lord?"

He smiled, a slightly wicked smile, that sent Patrice's heart into overdrive. "Call me anything you like, darlin'. Just don't call me late for supper."

A nervous laugh escaped her. She'd been afraid his wicked smile meant she'd planted visions of servant-master games in his mind, but instead he'd been gearing up to zap her with an old joke.

It seemed she was the only one having visions of herself in a Victorian dress with an apron and bonnet, waiting to do his bidding. Knowing that no matter what he asked her to do, she would do it because her job and livelihood depended on her pleasing him.

"Sorry, I couldn't resist," he said.

She had to return his smile—it was impossible not to. Before she did something totally crazy—like launch herself across the couch and into his arms for the kiss she'd been denied this afternoon—she opened her book and began to read.

* * *

Stone glanced up from his book again. He was having trouble concentrating. His gaze kept straying to Patrice. At the moment her head was tilted to the side, resting on the arm of the couch and her eyes were closed. Her book, still open, was lying beside her.

The lamp behind them on the table, turned bright so they could read, created a halo effect around her. While the rosy glow from the fireplace danced over her delicate features.

He swore beneath his breath as he felt his body respond to the sight of her. He'd spent a major part of the day alternating from partially to fully aroused...and it was starting to get painful.

Speaking of pain, Patrice was going to wake with a pain in her neck if she stayed in that position for much longer. He got up quietly, went over to the bunk and fixed her sleeping bag and pillow for the night.

Returning to the couch, he tried to rouse her, but she only mumbled and snuggled deeper into the cushions. The sexy wiggle sent another bolt of desire straight through him.

In a flash he scooped her into his arms and headed for the bed. She snuggled against him as she'd snuggled into the couch, causing him to swear again and question the wisdom of having her in his arms.

He placed her on the sleeping bag, carefully slipped off her boots, then zipped her in.

Her red-gold hair spread across the white of the pillowcase, reminding him of an angel. Looking down at her, he wondered what kind of man she'd been engaged to. Some suited Wall Street type, no doubt. He could picture Patrice meeting the man at the door, handing him a glass of white wine and slowly undoing his tie.

She hadn't said much about the breakup, but he'd seen a flash of pain in her eyes. Whatever had happened to end the relationship had hurt her. He wondered how long they'd known each other and how long they'd been engaged.

Though he didn't know her well, he knew that any man who would let her get away was a fool. She deserved more.

All things considered, she was handling their current situation better than he'd expected. He'd been prepared for her to whine and complain. She hadn't. He had to chuckle when remembering how she would do a visual check of the area before stepping out the doorway and another before leaving the porch. She overdid it a bit, but it was good that she took a cautious approach to wildlife.

As he stood watching, her eyes fluttered open and she glanced around.

"You fell asleep on the couch. I brought you to bed," he said.

"Thanks, Stone." Her voice was husky with sleep.

She looked up at him, her eyes sleepy and a faint smile curving her tempting lips. Lips he wanted so much to taste.

He'd found the strength to resist that temptation earlier, but did he have the strength to do it again?

Four

Patrice's eyelids felt as though they were weighed down, but she fought to keep them open. Surely no dream she might sink into could be half as wonderful as the sight of Stone leaning over her.

His features started to blur. A soft gasp escaped her lips when she realized the reason. He was going to kiss her.

His lips were warm…no, hot…so hot compared to the cold air in the cabin. He tasted of coffee. The scent of wood smoke lingered on his skin. His beard was as soft against her cheeks as it had been to her fingers earlier.

Dazed, Patrice returned the kiss. Scooting closer

to the edge of the bunk, she reached her arms around his neck to pull him nearer. Parting her lips slightly so she could taste even more.

Heat exploded, then settled into a constant burn when Stone parted his as well, increasing the intimacy by teasing with his tongue. He teased and tempted until she responded by mirroring his motions. Then he thrust deeper, tasting her and sending her pulse and nerve endings on a mad, wild rush of pleasure.

Never in her wildest fantasies had she imagined a kiss could feel so good. A shudder passed through her.

His hair curled over her fingers. The texture surprisingly soft...much softer than it looked. She trailed her fingers through it again and again.

Long, mind-blowing moments later, Stone ended the kiss and straightened to his full height. He looked down at her. In the dim light, she couldn't read the expression on his face.

She moved one hand to her bottom lip, touching where his lips had caressed only seconds before.

He tucked a strand of hair behind her ear. ''Should I apologize?''

She turned her head to rest her cheek against his hand. ''Only if you're sorry.''

''Not in the least. Are you?''

She should be...her logical side cried out. ''It was just a good-night kiss,'' she said.

And pigs fly, Patrice.

"All right. Good night, then."

"Good night."

He turned and headed to the couch. Patrice lowered her eyelids, but left enough room beneath so she could watch him. Watch him and marvel at the magic that had so briefly flared between them.

Her heart thudded in her chest. She wanted more....

What was happening to her all of a sudden? She had enjoyed prolonged bouts of necking on the couch with her early boyfriends, and her ex-fiancé's kisses had been all right. But she'd never felt tempted to change her mind about waiting until after the wedding before making love for the first time. She had assumed that when the honeymoon came, she would feel the desire to go further. But maybe that had been nothing more than false hopes.

She had never believed in the concept of instant physical sparks between two people. But that was before Stone had kissed her. And before she experienced it firsthand.

Deep inside, she knew that if he had been the one she'd been engaged to, there would have been no question of waiting.

Why was she having these physical desires...now...after all these years and with a perfect stranger to boot! Perfect, the word had special meaning when applied to Stone. She watched him as he sat staring into the fire, rubbing his fingers over his beard.

What was he thinking?

He'd said he wasn't sorry that he'd kissed her, but had he said so only to spare her feelings? Had he somehow sensed the strangely marvelous manner in which his kiss had affected her? How had it felt to him...different and special in any way? Or was it just another kiss?

He started to look her way. Quickly she closed her eyes, pretending to sleep.

She knew it would be a long, long time before sleep would come for her. There were too many questions on her mind to keep her awake. Not to mention the lingering taste of him in her mouth and on her lips.

Stone gazed into the fire.

So much for good intentions, buddy.

A sinking feeling had settled into the pit of his stomach the moment he knew he couldn't resist taking a small taste of her.

It wasn't the first time he'd kissed a woman since Val's death, but it was the first time he'd had such a quick, strong physical response. Even when he'd initiated a kiss knowing full well that taking the woman to bed was a done deal, desire hadn't grabbed him so hard and fast.

He didn't dare touch Patrice again....

Unless he could be sure she wanted him as much as he wanted her. There was the whole matter of her recent breakup. Was there truth to the saying that a jilted woman was on the rebound and would be easy pickings?

If it was true, he knew he couldn't take advantage of her that way. No matter how much his body craved hers.

His first reaction at the end of the kiss had been the urge to apologize. They didn't know each other well, and she'd been half-asleep. But her remark that he should only apologize if he were sorry made it clear to him that he wasn't sorry...not that he'd kissed her.

He was only sorry that he couldn't allow himself to let it progress to anything beyond mere kisses.

There was only one way to be certain he didn't act against his better judgment. That was to keep as far away from her as possible.

When Patrice awoke, once again Stone was already up. She realized she hadn't felt or heard him come to bed last night. Probably for the best, after their kiss she was so aware of him, she might not have been able to get back to sleep once she knew he was lying in the bunk below.

Stone was putting more logs in the stove as she climbed down from the bunk.

"Good morning," he said. "Did you sleep well?"

"Yes, did you?"

He glanced to the side. "Sure, I slept just fine."

His voice seemed a bit gruffer this morning. Maybe he wasn't a morning person. How would she know? This was only the second morning they'd been together.

The intimacy of the situation struck her again...catching her blind side. Quickly she put on her boots, jacket, hat and gloves and made her morning trip out back. She couldn't be completely sure, but it seemed to her that the air was a bit warmer and the snowflakes were starting to fall in a more calm, orderly fashion.

When she returned to the cabin, the first thing she noticed was that Stone had opened the shutters on the front windows. It was amazing what a little extra light did to brighten up the plain surroundings.

Plain, but not unpleasant.

In her mind's eye she could picture the scene with a bouquet of wildflowers sprouting from the blue enamel coffeepot sitting in the middle of the table. The flowers would have been picked in the meadow, of course. And there would be so many more scattered among the green grass that it would be impossible to tell where the bouquet had been plucked.

"Ready for breakfast?" Stone asked.

She didn't feel hungry, but it was morning and by rights she should be. "Yes."

Her cheeks felt warm…a combination of the difference in the temperature between inside and outside and the hint of a blush as she replayed last night's kiss in her mind. Thank heavens he couldn't read her thoughts.

Anyone looking in on them would never believe the sparks that had passed between them last night. It was hard for her to believe the kiss even happened. Maybe she'd imagined the whole thing. Or dreamed it.

Conversation over breakfast was almost nonexistent. After they had eaten and cleaned up, Stone used the cellular phone to once again call the man he called Mack.

He muttered an expletive as he set the phone down on the table.

"Problems?"

He rubbed his hand across the back of his neck. "Storm damage, but no more than expected."

Patrice's fingertips tingled as she thought about how his warm skin had felt last night. But she couldn't let her thoughts stray in that direction too long.

The rest of the day passed slowly. Stone was polite, but the blossoming mutual awareness and whatever rapport had been building between them yesterday was gone. She told herself she should be glad the awareness was gone, but felt safe in allowing herself to miss the rapport.

By late afternoon the wind had died down even more, and the snow had stopped although the sky remained a steel gray.

"It looks like the storm is over," she said.

"Yes, it does. Tomorrow I'll take a walk and check out the condition of the road."

The thought of getting out of the cabin for a while pleased her. "Could I go with you?"

"I don't see why not...as long as you bundle up."

"Think we'll be able to leave soon?"

He ran his fingers through his hair. "I'll have a better idea tomorrow. In a hurry to leave?"

"I'm sure you must be, too."

By all rights she should be, but was she really? The peaceful retreat had to come to an end eventually, but was she ready to give it up?

Of course she couldn't hide here forever. Although that would certainly be one solution to all her problems. There was an appeal to never going back to the real world...never having to face rebuilding her life.

Her mental revelry stopped when she realized that when she pictured herself staying here, she pictured Stone being with her.

One kiss and he was firmly established in her fantasy.

The mountain cabin had been a blessing in disguise. Absolutely the only thing she wanted beyond this place was to see her grandmother. Going back to Phoenix had no appeal for her. All that remained there were the tatters of her old life.

But soon she would have to go back and face it again. The escape had been unexpected and wonderful, but it was about to come to an end. Sadness and regret threatened to swamp her emotions, but she pushed them aside so she could enjoy what little time she had left.

Stone kept himself busy the rest of the day at the table writing in a small notebook he'd pulled out of his jacket pocket and reading his book. Patrice sat on the couch reading. She was halfway through the suspense novel and wanted to be sure she finished it before they left.

Every few pages, her gaze drifted to Stone. She wondered why he didn't join her on the couch as he had yesterday. Despite her resolve not to let it, her mind drifted to thoughts of the kiss they'd shared.

Now that some of the surprise was wearing off, she began to wonder why he had kissed her. He'd never answered yesterday when she'd asked why he wanted to.

She knew he was a widower, but did he date? Did he have a steady girlfriend?

She wanted to know…wanted to ask, but what difference would his answers make?

None. However, her strong reaction to him still troubled her.

Neil's kisses had been pleasant, but never left her yearning for more. She could still hear his voice as he ended his good-night kisses. "That's all for now, hon. We'll wait. I respect you too much."

Respect…ha! The man had been plotting to rob her blind, so he obviously didn't respect her.

Which made her wonder. If he didn't respect her, then why hadn't he made love to her? They'd been engaged. Many engaged couples slept together. So why had it been so easy for Neil to resist her?

The answer seemed painfully obvious…because she was undesirable. There had never been a long line of men queuing up to pursue her. Maybe she didn't have that sexual spark that drew men.

Stone had managed not to kiss her yesterday afternoon. The kiss later may have been a fluke.

She glanced down at her oversize, borrowed clothing and had to fight back a sigh. No way, nohow would Stone be interested in her.

They went through the rest of the day and night as polite strangers.

The next morning, Stone set about getting breakfast ready. His gaze occasionally drifted to Patrice, still sleeping in her bunk.

He wished his sleep had been so peaceful. His dreams had been full of Val and the too-brief love they'd shared.

With the visions still fresh in his mind it was hard not to dwell on the emptiness of his life and the fear that he would spend the rest of his life alone. Usually work at the ranch kept him so busy he didn't have time to think of it, let alone dwell on it.

But he had too much time on his hands here. Way too much time...

Patrice stirred and sighed in her sleep. What dreams was she dreaming? Was she dreaming of her ex? The jerk didn't deserve any of her time— sleeping or otherwise.

Easy, pal, you don't have any idea what you're talking about.

He didn't have a clue as to what had happened between them. All he knew was that the guy had hurt her. And while he didn't know her well, she seemed like a nice lady who deserved someone better.

As he watched, her eyes opened. They opened but remained unfocused at first. He could tell the moment she came fully awake. A smile curved her lips.

"Good morning," she said, her voice husky from sleep.

"Mornin'."

She scooted out of the sleeping bag and sat up. With one hand she tucked her hair behind her ears. It was tousled, but he liked it. He knew it had gotten that way merely from her sleeping, but it was easy to picture the strands sliding through his fingers as he leaned over her.

The jolt to his body was swift and fierce. That single image was followed by others...his fingers undoing the buttons of her shirt, sliding it off her, lifting the thermal shirt over her head. And that image left him wondering what kind of bra was she wearing? Color? Material?

"Stone?" The sound of her voice broke into his thoughts.

"What?"

"I asked if you'd checked the weather yet today."

"Um, yes, I have. The storm seems to have blown itself out."

A strange, unreadable look passed over her features, before she smiled again. "Not much longer then, and you can get back to work."

"And you can get to your grandmother's."

"I'm looking forward to seeing her."

He wondered if she was looking forward to getting rid of him.

Patrice moved to the bottom of the bunk. He could see only the faintest outline of her backside beneath the baggy jeans as she climbed down, but it was enough to send his thoughts reeling again. Making him wish his own blue jeans were a little on the baggy side, too.

Damn, what had come over him this morning!

But then it wasn't just this morning…hadn't it really gotten started the day before yesterday when he'd started having the uncontrollable urge to kiss her?

And giving in to the urge had only made the problem worse. Now he was really suffering!

He watched her bundle up into the jacket and outside gear for her morning trip to the outhouse. Since that first evening, she hadn't voiced the smallest complaint about the accommodations.

In fact, if it wasn't for his body's annoying reaction to her, he would be enjoying her company.

He had breakfast ready by the time she got back. They ate, and then worked together cleaning up. She was putting the bowls away on one shelf when he walked to the cupboard and set the coffeepot on the shelf above that.

She turned. He knew she was expecting him to step back and let her pass. He knew he should do that. And he almost did.

But instead he took a step closer, bringing his body next to hers. Wrapping his arms around her, he moved them even closer together. Her muscles tensed and she stiffened in his arms. Before she could protest, he leaned forward and kissed her.

It was pure heaven, the warmth and moistness of her mouth as his tongue slipped past her lips. He could feel the tenseness leaving her muscles as she relaxed against him and gave in to the kiss. This time he knew her reaction wasn't exaggerated because she was half-asleep and not aware of what she was doing.

The soft press of her feminine curves against his chest took his breath away. With her coloring, he pictured shell pink nipples against the fairness of her skin. They would be pulled tight from the cold. He would warm them with his mouth, covering each in turn, sucking gently.

Her arms came up around his neck, breaking his thoughts, but sending a shiver of desire through him as her fingers curled into his hair. His scalp tingled where she touched it and in ever widening circles beyond.

She moved closer, snuggling against him, and he thought he would explode then and there. Moving his hands down her back, he spanned her hips and pulled them tight against him. A shiver ripped through him.

Visions of the two of them naked, legs entwined, flashed into his mind, obliterating all other thoughts. He swept her into his arms and headed toward the bunk.

When he reached the beds, he put her down slowly, letting her body slide over his. He gasped when she brushed across the ache behind his blue jeans zipper. Burying a groan along the side of her neck, he kissed her there as well before straightening to look down at her.

Her eyes had that not quite focused look again as she returned his gaze. Reaching up, he ran one hand across her cheek, brushing her kiss-swollen lips with his thumb. The tip of her tongue slipped out to touch him.

Moving his hand to cradle her chin, he kissed her again. With his other hand, he caressed her back, then slid around to the curve of her full breast.

She tensed and broke the kiss. "I thought we were going out to check on the road today."

"This afternoon, when it's warmed up a bit. There are a number of hours between now and then, darlin'."

Five

A number of hours between now and then.

The thought of spending those hours in Stone's arms sent a flurry of excitement through Patrice's body.

But his remark also reminded her of the mental conversation she'd had with herself yesterday about her lack of desirability. She stiffened her spine even more. "Bored, Stone? Looking for a new way to pass the time?"

She pushed his chest, and he released his hold on her. Patrice jumped out of the bed.

"That's not what I meant," Stone said, following her. "I just wanted you to know we had plenty of time to linger, that it wouldn't be a rushed job."

She made a sound of disbelief and kept walking. Although with the limited space, she couldn't go far.

Stone continued, "I'll admit that I want to make love to you...and it's not because I'm bored. If you're honest, you'll admit you want me, too."

Admitting it to him wouldn't help matters—probably just feed his ego—so she didn't say a word. Admitting it to herself was another matter entirely, but one she chose not to explore at the moment.

"Then again," Stone said, "just because I don't think I'm bored doesn't mean a pillow made of horsefeathers. Being around you has my hormones so riled up, I can't see straight...let alone think."

His words summed up her feelings exactly.

They didn't speak again until after lunch, when Stone announced it was time to head outside and check the road conditions.

"Can I still go with you?" she asked.

"Sure. Bundle up."

She followed his advice, adding extra thermals and a sweater over her clothes. Once done, she was wearing so many extra layers she could barely bend her knees and elbows. Stone settled his cowboy hat on his head, then held the door open for her.

From the porch, she saw footprints in the snow from their trips out back and from Stone's trips to the woodpile, or to gather snow for wash water, but the main expanse of meadow was covered by an untouched blanket of white. It was so flat and perfect it looked more like a movie set than the real world.

"Be careful walking. There are a number of rocks and tree branches beneath the snow. In fact, your best bet would be to follow in my footsteps."

Patrice tried, but the width of his stride made it impossible. She used his prints when she could, but added her own in between.

In some places the snow was so deep, Patrice sank into calf-high holes. In others where the wind had blown the snow away, it was barely up to her ankles.

Stone pointed out deer, elk and rabbit tracks— left by unseen visitors.

They didn't have to go any great distance down the road leading away from the cabin to see that, even with four-wheel drive, they weren't likely to get far. The snowdrifts were banked against tree trunks, but spread across the narrow path. And since they'd come several miles up the hill, the thought of shoveling the way clear was out of the question. It would be springtime before they would reach the end.

From the grim set of Stone's jaw, she suspected her assessment of the situation was accurate.

He stood in the center of the road, his gloved

fists resting on his hips, his eyes focused down the mountain.

He turned and his gaze settled on her. Patrice caught her breath. She knew he was thinking about their kisses. Although she wasn't sure how she knew.

In a few strides he was next to her. "Feel up to a longer walk?"

They hadn't gone far, yet. "Sure." At least it would keep them out of the cabin and out of temptation.

He gestured to the left. "This way."

Patrice followed as Stone walked back up the road, across the meadow and up the path on the far side. The air was cold in her lungs, so cold it almost felt hot. But it felt good to be in wide-open spaces. She hadn't realized that she'd been starting to feel closed in. But from her joy at being outside, she suspected now that she had been. Maybe that was what was causing all the craziness over Stone kissing her.

Occasionally the weight of snow on the pine branches would send a shower of white to the ground. When one landed on Stone's shoulder, Patrice couldn't hold back a giggle.

Stone stopped and looked over his shoulder at her. "You think that was funny?"

She tried to rein in her smile. "Uh, no. Of course not."

He laughed, and she could see the gloomy mood lift from his rigid stance. "Right, darlin'. Like I'm going to believe that."

He kept his gaze on her, crouched down and gathered a handful of snow. She didn't have to be a "snowbunny" to know she was in trouble.

Patrice raced to duck behind the nearest tree, but before she got there, a snowball smacked into her shoulder, exploding into a shower of cold powder.

She tried to return the favor, but every snowball she made fell apart long before it got near Stone. By the time she gave up trying, he was laughing so hard he couldn't stand up straight.

Brushing off her gloves, as though she'd completed rather than failed at her task, she walked over to Stone and asked, "Where are we going?"

"There's something I want to show you."

They walked another ten minutes before reaching an area where the trees began to thin, and the ground sloped upward. Stone stopped ahead. Patrice followed to stand by his side.

Her breath caught in her throat at the view before them. They stood on a cliff overlooking a wide valley, stretching off to forever horizons where another set of rugged, tree-lined mountains rose to the sky. Everything was covered with pure white snow.

It looked like a fairy-tale kingdom.

"It's beautiful," Patrice said.

"It's always been one of my favorite spots. My

grandmother claims her grandmother told her this was one of her tribe's holy places.''

"The great-great-grandmother on the baron's side?''

"Yes, his wife.''

Patrice wasn't surprised to learn he had Native American ancestors. His dark hair and rugged cheekbones should have clued her in.

There was power of some kind in the place...whether from a divine source or simply from the size of the awe-inspiring vista. A calming peacefulness was working its way through her. She felt very small and insignificant in the big picture, but suddenly just being a part of the whole, no matter how small, seemed comforting.

She wrapped her arms across her chest, not so much from the cold, but more as a self hug.

They stood together appreciating the view, neither speaking.

Patrice looked up at Stone's profile. His face was shadowed beneath his hat, but she could see or maybe sense the tranquillity starting to soften the hard lines of his face. Once again she was struck by the rightness of him in his surroundings. This man belonged here.

"It does seem like a holy place. The space. The silence," she said.

Snow fell from a tree behind them making a splatting sound as it hit.

He turned and smiled at her. "Not completely silent."

"I broke the silence first, but then Mother Nature had to get her two cents worth in."

"Doesn't she always?"

Patrice shrugged. "I'm sure you would know more about that than I would. We don't notice nature much in the city, unless the weather does something very extreme."

"I think I would miss not being able to see all her glory and subtleties."

She looked out at the snowy valley and wondered if in the future she would long for such a sight in wintertime. "If you'd never known them, you wouldn't know what you were missing. I suppose you have all four seasons up here?"

"Definitely."

"I've never seen all four seasons in a row. And never seen a *real* winter until now."

"You're getting a firsthand taste of winter at its harshest."

When they'd arrived it had been harsh, but now it didn't seem as threatening. "It has mellowed over the last few days."

"Yes, it has. For the moment."

She hadn't considered it, but, yes, winter probably was more than one big storm. "It might be cold, but it really is beautiful."

"Beautiful. But dangerous. You shouldn't underestimate the danger.'' His voice took on a different tone, sounding far away. As though he wasn't talking about winter anymore. What could he possibly mean instead?

Patrice looked back across the valley and spotted a curving line working its way across it. ''Is there a river down there?''

''Yes. It starts up here. There's a waterfall behind the next ridge that gets it to the valley.''

''I'm surprised it's not frozen.''

''Parts of it probably are, but most times there's at least a small trickle of the waterfall and river that keep moving.''

A gentle breeze lifted the ends of her scarf and slid under the hem of her jacket. She shivered and tucked her gloved hands into her pockets.

''We should be getting back,'' Stone said.

''It's so beautiful, I hate to leave, but it is awfully cold.''

On the walk to the cabin, Stone led the way again, until Patrice tripped over a buried rock and started to fall. Then he took her arm to guide her. The feeling of comfort the view had inspired in her increased. She glanced at the cowboy by her side. Suddenly he seemed taller, stronger. A man to look up to, a man to lend a hand in hard times...not so much by his actions, but simply by his presence.

She could almost picture him as the perfect big brother. If only she could banish the thought of their kisses. Those were certainly not brotherly. Walking so close to him, it was hard not to think about them and think about him kissing her again...or making love to her.

Get a grip, Patrice! Didn't you learn anything from the Neil experience? Men cannot be trusted! Even though Stone seemed like a nice guy....

She couldn't let stray thoughts of Stone become an obsession.

Soon they would be leaving. She wondered if she would ever see him again once they left the cabin. Would he kiss her goodbye?

It seemed unlikely. And it definitely was silly for her to worry about such things. After all they were two strangers who happened to have been stranded together. Sure, they'd talked, but hardly enough to make them best friends...or even good friends.

And it was still a possibility that he had a steady girlfriend wherever home was.

The trek back seemed longer than the walk to the overlook, even though she knew it was the same distance because they followed their own footprints.

Despite the energy she was expending to walk through the deep snow, her feet were starting to feel colder, and the shivers were intensifying.

By the time they reached the cabin, her teeth were chattering uncontrollably, and she felt the cold deep in her bones. Even more than she had on the day they'd arrived. And that had been the coldest she'd felt in her life.

The first thing Stone did was to build up the fire. Patrice stood as close as was safe, holding her hands out in front of her.

She was still shivering when Stone brought her a cup of coffee he'd warmed on the stove.

"Here, try this."

She took it, wrapping her fingers around the mug. It was hard taking a sip without spilling while her teeth clicked together. The liquid was warm, but it only made a small dent in the vast coldness that gripped her.

"Could I make a suggestion?" Stone asked.

She looked up at the tall, virile cowboy who'd propositioned her that morning. Through chattering teeth, she said, "Don't even think about suggesting that we get naked and share body heat!"

Six

Stone's mouth quirked up in a half smile. "As enjoyable as that sounds, darlin', I was going to suggest we put an extra set of clothes near the fire to warm them. Then they'll be nice and toasty so you can change into them."

Patrice felt the blood rush to her cheeks.

Stone walked to the dresser and the cupboard, gathering up the garments. He carried one of the benches from the table and set it in front of the fireplace. Then he laid the clothes on top. Next he brought her sleeping bag, opening it to warm as well.

Talk about putting your foot in your mouth, Patrice.

She took a sip of the coffee, then set the mug on the mantel before continuing to hold her hands in front of the fire, watching the flames dance so she wouldn't look at Stone.

Maybe she had been right when she'd thought earlier that he'd wanted to make love to her for something to do…and now the mood had passed.

After ten minutes, they turned the heating items over to warm the other side.

Ten minutes after that, Stone said, ''They should be ready. I'll be back in fifteen minutes.''

''All right.''

Why was he leaving? Last time she'd changed, he'd simply turned his back. She should be grateful for the extra privacy, but ironically she found herself wondering about his reasons. Did he think he'd be more tempted to look this time?

In a way, she hoped that was the case. It would mean she wasn't completely undesirable.

Give it a rest, hon.

Her desirability shouldn't be at question here; it was strictly an ego issue set off by Neil's behavior and betrayal. It was something she was going to have to deal with, but it had nothing to do with Stone. After all, they were only ships passing in the night. Two people thrown together for a few days' time.

As soon as the door closed behind him, she began to change. Stripping down to her bare skin sent another round of shivers racing through her, but when she pulled on the warmed garments they began to soothe at once.

She stayed close to the fire. Retrieving her mug from the mantel, she sipped her coffee. Slowly she felt the warmth of the clothes begin to fade, some of it soaking into her, some being lost to the room.

After setting down her mug, she picked up the sleeping bag and wrapped it around her shoulders.

The door opened a crack and Stone called to her, "All clear?"

"Yes. Come on in."

He stomped his boots then came through the doorway. After taking off his outerwear and hanging it up, he walked over to her.

"Did that help?"

"It felt great at first, but now I'm getting cool again."

He came up behind her, wrapped his arms around her waist and pulled her against him. His shoulders curled forward making her feel snug and protected. Almost immediately she felt warmer, even through all the clothing and the sleeping bag.

She stayed there for a moment, allowing herself the comfort, then turned to look up at him.

He smiled. "Is it helping?"

"Actually it is."

"Good."

Slowly he lowered his head toward her until their

lips met. He'd just come in from outside, so by rights his lips should be colder than hers. But they weren't.

His hands came up to her shoulders and turned her around until they were face-to-face. He continued kissing her, and she snuggled against his hard length. She opened to the warmth of him. And the warmth wasn't only where their lips met, nor where she rested against him—it was starting to seep through her whole body.

Stone moved his mouth from hers and began a trail of kisses down her neck. She reached up and tangled her hands in his hair and felt the sleeping bag start to slip. It didn't go far, held in place by the crush of their bodies.

A sigh escaped her as he lingered on her sensitive pulse. When he opened his mouth to run his tongue over it, a shiver ran down her spine.

"Still cold, darlin'? Would you like more coffee?"

"I'm, ah, not shivering from the cold."

He straightened and looked down at her, smiling. "Bored, Patrice?"

She felt a blush creep up her cheeks. "No, I'm not bored."

"And boredom has nothing to do with the reasons I want to make love to you. I want you because holding you, kissing you affects me physically. And I want to kiss you because I know how good it feels.''

"Me, too, but I don't understand why. Could it be cabin fever?''

"I've had cabin fever before. A restless, trapped feeling, but it's never had this type of impact on me.'' He ran his hand over her cheek. "I can't even begin to tell you how much I want you.''

A throbbing ache started between her legs in response to his words and the hot look of desire in his eyes. After the torturous thoughts of doubting her desirability, his obvious longing soothed her soul. That rat Neil might not have wanted her, but Stone did.

He wanted her and the knowledge was so much more than she'd imagined in her dreams and fantasies the first night at the cabin.

Suddenly a small voice whispered that giving in to their wants might not be such a good idea. They would be parting soon and didn't even live in the same state. But for the first time in her life, she didn't want to listen to the voice of fear and reason.

He wanted her. She wanted him. And for the moment, that's all that mattered. That was all she would let be important.

"I want you, too, Stone.''

His chest expanded as he took a deep breath, pressing his body more tightly against hers.

He took her mouth again in a sweet kiss. One

that acknowledged the mutual longing they had spoken to each other and promised to fulfill that longing.

She felt him untangle the sleeping bag and let it drop to the floor. Gathering her in his arms, he pulled her close. The magic of his lips moving over hers continued.

Hazily she felt him slip his hands between them and start working the buttons on her shirt free of their holes. She caught her breath. Even though there was still the layer of thermal underwear separating their touch, she had a fleeting glimpse of what it would feel like when he made contact with her bare skin—a moment she was suddenly impatient for.

Trailing her hands over his shoulders and across his chest, she began opening his buttons. Her fingers trembled slightly, making it harder than it should be.

Stone was also wearing thermals beneath his shirt. Her knuckles brushed against them as she worked her way down. He had his shirt tucked in, so she stopped when she reached the waistband of his jeans. Splaying her hands over the hard wall of his stomach, she felt a ripple run through his muscles.

He broke the kiss and reached down to untuck his shirttails, then opened his hands around her waist. Patrice finished off the buttons, holding the bottom folds of the heavy flannel in her hands.

She felt a brief second of panic when she realized she didn't know what to do next, but then he smiled and all panic fled. Smiling back, she began to take off his shirt. He did the same with hers.

"Hang on a sec," he said.

Reaching down, he spread the sleeping bag in front of the fireplace, then brought the pillows from the bunks. Taking her hand, he lowered himself to the floor, pulling her with him.

He moved his hands under her thermal top. Patrice caught her breath at the pure sensation. Suddenly all thoughts of being cold escaped her mind. His skin was warm against her, and the roughness of his hands attested to the hard work they performed on a regular basis.

Slowly he moved them over her, skimming her back, sliding to the front. With fingers splayed, he worked his way upward until his hands covered her breasts. Her quick inhale pushed them even more firmly into his grasp.

His eyes closed as his caress increased in intimacy, his thumbs brushing across her nipples. A soft growl of male appreciation escaped his parted lips. The essence of her femininity responded to it...the call of her mate.

In one smooth motion, he swept the thermal shirt over her head and to the ground behind them, exposing her pale pink lace-and-satin bra. With his fingertips, he teased along the lacy edges and watched as her already aroused nipples pushed even tighter against the fabric covering them.

Leaning forward he continued the sweet torment with his mouth. Her whole body was trembling by the time he stopped and reached behind her to release the hook.

This time when he growled, his open mouth was on her bare skin, and she felt as well as heard it. He kissed and caressed her until every nerve ending hummed with longing.

She didn't think she could feel any better, but then he removed his thermal shirt and closed the distance between them.

"Sweet heaven," the words escaped him in a rush.

On the first day when he'd swept her into his arms, she'd gotten the impression of a rock-hard body. The brief glimpse she'd caught and the sensation of his skin against hers proved how right she'd been. The dusting of dark hair brushed against her aroused nipples, adding to the pleasure.

She sighed, and he caught the sound in his mouth. Wrapping her arms tightly around him, she let the new sensations fill her. One of his jean-clad legs moved between hers. She could feel his arousal against her hip. There was no doubt that he wanted her.

He tugged at the rope holding her blue jeans, untying it. Patrice reached for his belt buckle. Following his lead, piece by piece, she helped dispose of the rest of their clothing. She expected to be cold, but as Stone's gaze moved over her, she felt a heat wave sweep across her skin.

The heat banished any embarrassment or shyness. And the sight of Stone…that was enough to steal her breath from her lungs.

He held her gently, tucking her close to his body. Letting his fingers trail over her, he watched her reactions closely. When he moved his caresses below her waist, he leaned forward and kissed her.

She kissed him back, opening her mouth, yielding, giving him free access. When he slid his hand even lower, she yielded to him again, letting him touch her in intimate ways no other man ever had.

Each touch built upon the one before, adding to the passion burning between them.

When at last he knelt between her knees, Patrice didn't know where she was, what day of the week or even what season. All she knew was the reality of the man above her. In a daze she watched him retrieve his jeans, get his wallet and retrieve a condom. He slipped it on, then eased down to align their bodies so he could enter her. Slowly he began to join them. There was a tightness, then a twinge of pain.

He stopped immediately, leaned up on his elbows and looked at her. "Patrice?"

"Um, Stone?"

"Oh, darlin', don't tell me this is your first time."

How could she tell him that she'd completely forgotten? That she'd been so focused on what he made her feel that she'd thought of nothing else beyond having him make love to her. "All right. I won't tell you."

He buried his head against the curve of her neck and swore softly. She waited for him to move away, but he remained still.

Skimming her hands across his back, she reached up and cradled the back of his head, entwining her fingers in his hair. Sure that he would pull back any second, she tried to commit every detail of the moment to memory. The feel of him against her...the warmth and weight. The scent of him, the aftertaste of his kiss. The steady beat of his heart against her, the rise and fall of his chest with each breath he took. The texture of his hair running through her fingers.

All of this she would tuck away so she would have it to remember. A reminder of the first time she had almost been loved by a man.

He stirred in her arms. She loosened her hold, and he leaned up on his elbows.

"I wish you had told me."

"I was preoccupied."

He shook his head. "Darlin', a woman's first time shouldn't be on the floor of a line shack."

"And where should it be? In a bed with silk sheets?"

"Yes...but if not, then in a bed at the very least."

"Let's move to the bunk." She started to push up.

"Don't...move," Stone's voice was tense, his words coming from between clenched teeth.

She could feel the tension in his muscles as he fought for control. But she didn't want him in·control...she wanted him out of control.

If they took the time to move to the bunk, it would give him time and space to change his mind. They'd come this far, and she wanted them to go the rest of the way.

She ignored his request, running her hands over his shoulders and rocking her hips against him. Small movements, but enough to push him over the edge.

With a groan, he pulled back slightly, then drove hard and fast into her, joining them completely. Patrice gasped. The pain was sharp, but brief. A strange sensation of pleasure followed.

"You all right?" Stone asked.

She smiled. "I am."

And she was. She felt warm, safe and fully alive for perhaps the first time in her life.

Once again Stone turned his concentration to her body, touching, tasting. He began to move, long slow strokes that sent ripples of pleasure raging through her. She closed her eyes and floated on the joy of it.

When he increased the tempo, she felt her heart-beat and breathing speed up as well. A spiraling tension began to build deep within her. It grew in strength until she felt the first flutter and then a rush of uncontrollable contractions. She cried out from the wonder of it.

Stone took his own release mere moments after her. She was stunned by the powerful intensity of his reaction, holding him tightly to her until the last shudders passed through him.

He kissed her briefly, then shifted to his side, pulling her close and wrapping the sleeping bag around them. Patrice snuggled against him, laying her cheek on his chest. She felt the soft touch of a kiss on her hair.

The flames danced in the fireplace. Slowly, they began to hypnotize her. Between the flames, the gentle rise and fall of Stone breathing, the soothing caress of his hand across her back and the languid relaxation seeping through her body, she drifted to sleep.

* * *

Stone rested his chin on top of Patrice's head. Her hair curled softly against his cheek. From her stillness and the slow rhythm of her breathing, he was fairly certain she was asleep.

He couldn't believe she'd been a virgin. She wasn't a kid, and she'd been engaged to be married.

He hoped once she awoke she wouldn't regret what they'd done. He wondered why she'd chosen to give her virginity to him. Had she simply been swept up in the same tide of desire that had gotten hold of him?

Maybe it was some strange kind of cabin fever that the two of them created in each other. Heaven knew he'd never experienced anything like it before. When she'd said she was a virgin, he'd fully intended to stop and go no further. If she'd kept still, he might have succeeded, but she'd wiggled and sent him racing full speed ahead.

And she'd been right with him every step of the way....

She was incredibly responsive and that had rocked him from head to toes.

Running his hands over the skin of her back, he marveled at the smooth softness of it. He turned his head to watch the flames. They reminded him of the highlights that danced in Patrice's hair.

He took a deep breath and let it out slowly. A half smile curved his lips. He realized how good he felt...how at peace. It was a settling feeling he hadn't experienced in a long time. So long he hadn't recognized it at first.

The feeling that he wanted this moment to last forever…lying here holding Patrice in his arms. What a treasure she was, this warm, trusting woman nestled against him.

Too bad she lived so far away. He could definitely get used to having her around.

Patrice woke slowly. The first thing she noticed was the encompassing heat surrounding her. It felt so good to be warm after the cold of the cabin.

The cabin? When had she left the cabin? Her eyes flew open. She saw immediately that she was still in the cabin and remembered the source of the warmth. Stone.

The sun had set while she'd slept, and since they hadn't lit the lanterns, only the lingering flames in the fireplace lit the room, cloaking everything with a rosy tinge.

She turned her head to look at Stone. His eyes were closed.

As she watched, they opened. She remembered her first impression of his eyes…about the incredible shade of blue and about how seductive they were. She'd well and truly fallen into their spell.

"Hi." His voice was husky with sleep.

She smiled at him. "Hi."

His arms tightened around her. "How are you feeling?"

Like I've died and gone to heaven!

"Fine. Sorry I fell asleep."

"Hey, I did, too." His hands made circular patterns over her back. "Are you sure you're all right?"

"Stone, I'm fine."

"It's just that a woman's first time is usually with a fiancé or a steady boyfriend or..."

She felt blood rush to her cheeks. "I know."

"I'd assumed that since you'd been engaged..."

"A logical assumption."

"But not true in this case," he said, wiser now.

"No, we'd decided to wait until our honeymoon."

"Hell, Patrice, why did you let me..." He paused. "Why did you let me make love to you?"

"I guess that saying it seemed like a good idea at the time sounds rather lame."

"Is that why?"

How could she answer that? How could she tell him what he made her feel? About her fantasy of the two of them staying in the cabin forever. It was way too soon for her to be falling in love again...and they'd only just met!

"I wish I knew. You're an incredibly attractive man. We've been alone together for several days. And strange things happen inside me when you're near, and especially when we touch. One of those, maybe, or a combination?''

"Most women want declarations of love and commitment before they make love.''

"I know, and I've always thought I was that kind of woman, but I guess not.''

Neil's declarations of love and commitment had proven to be bellows of hot air.

Stone placed his hand under her chin, tilting her face toward him. "It may be the forced isolation. Cabin fever does strange things to people. Although I've never had this particular reaction to it.''

His words made her feel slightly more at ease in what was an awkward and uncomfortable situation.

A log shifted on the fire, sending up a handful of sparks.

"I should get more logs,'' Stone said.

Patrice started to slide out of the sleeping bag, but he pulled her back into his arms for a kiss first. His physical reaction was clear as they lay nestled together. A self-satisfied feeling burst inside her. It meant so much knowing this man wanted her again.

He took another condom from his wallet and loved her again. More gently this time…slower… drawing the feelings out.…

Their mutual passion burned hot, and they once again reached their peaks almost simultaneously.

Afterward, Stone dressed and headed outside to gather more wood.

Patrice took the opportunity of his absence to wash up as best she could before getting dressed, then lit the lanterns and started dinner. Once Stone returned, he added wood to the fires. Dinner was like all the other meals they'd shared, but the atmosphere in the room, the energy around them sizzled. They laughed, exchanged smiles and languid glances. Stone smiled and laughed more than he had in the last few days combined.

Once the dishes were done, Patrice headed out back. She noticed the moon peeking between the branches of the trees. Large and white, it scattered a blue-white glow over the snow. Tiny sparkles of light danced across the field, twinkling like fairy lights.

When she returned to the cabin, Stone was staring into the fire, a grim look on his face.

"Bad news from the ranch?"

What else could have changed his mood so quickly?

"No, I haven't talked to the ranch."

"Is something wrong? Did I do or say—"

He walked over to her, placing one finger over her lips. "Shh, you haven't done or said anything wrong." Reaching into the pocket of his jeans, he pulled out a foil packet. "Last one, darlin'."

Seven

Patrice felt the blood rush to her cheeks as a sinking feeling settled in the pit of her stomach. "Last one."

Stone nodded. "Last one."

It wasn't as though they could pop over to the drugstore for more. "Oh."

"We'll be here another few days at least." He turned and met her gaze. "I won't pretend it's going to be easy for me to keep my hands off you."

The thought of having him touch her was appealing. "And I won't pretend that I don't want them on me. But…"

"Yeah, I know." He looked down at the packet

in his hand. "Question is…do we use it now or save it?"

She would love to be in his arms right now, making love again. But then the long days ahead would stretch before them…and the long nights. Catching her bottom lip between her teeth, she shrugged.

"We should wait." He tucked the packet into the pocket of his flannel shirt and reached one arm toward her. "Come here, darlin'."

She went to him and he wrapped his arms around her, holding her close.

He laughed, deep in his chest, a laugh she felt through her soul. "Maybe I should add condoms to the line shack supply list. Or start carrying more."

A sliver of sadness passed through her as she wondered what lucky woman would be the next one to be stranded here with Stone. Chances were slim that it would be her. She wasn't sure, but the emotion rolling through her felt suspiciously like jealousy.

What's with you, Patrice?

It seemed so irrational. She hardly knew the man, and she was jealous of the future women in his life. Of course, he *was* her first lover. And he always would be her first lover. She supposed that distinction could account for the jealous feelings and maybe for the fact that she felt as though she was falling in love with him.

He kissed the top of her head. "But if we started

stocking condoms up here, we'd have every hot-blooded teenager in the county raiding the stash.''

She chuckled. ''And that could get expensive…not at all cost-effective.''

''Not at all.''

He moved his hands slowly across her back. She closed her eyes, resting against him. Moving one of his hands below her chin, he tipped her face up toward his.

''Want to play cribbage?'' he asked.

''Not really.'' She wasn't the least bit interested in playing cards, or doing anything for that matter, except being in Stone's arms. Even if they didn't make love tonight she wanted to be close to him. ''But I will if you want to.''

''I'm not exactly in a cribbage mood.''

Patrice bit her tongue to keep from asking what kind of mood he *was* in. If he said he wanted to make love, how could she tell him no? Even though she thought it was probably best that they wait until they couldn't wait any longer. She didn't question how she knew that moment would come, but she knew it would.

He wove one hand through her hair. ''Let's sit on the couch for a while.''

Stone sat in one corner, turned sideways to stretch what would fit of his long legs along the couch's cushions. Once settled, he pulled her into his lap.

She lay down along the length of him, her back against his chest, her head tucked under his chin, his arms encircling her. Settling in, she watched the fire dance in the fireplace. Stone kissed the top of her head again.

"Shall we read?" he asked.

"All right."

He reached beside the couch and picked up the books they'd been reading yesterday. Patrice opened hers and held it in front of her. Stone opened his and rested it on the arm of the couch. From the long, drawn-out pauses between his turning the pages, she was certain he was having as hard a time concentrating as she was.

Finally she gave up the pretense and closed the book, holding it against her chest.

He shifted slightly behind her. "Done?"

"No, I think I'll watch the fire for a while."

"I used to love watching the fire, looking for shapes in the flames."

"I used to do that with clouds."

"I did it with clouds, too, when I was younger."

"What was it like growing up on a ranch?" she asked.

"I liked it. But I'm not sure whether I'd have liked it better than anything else, because it's all I knew. Sometimes I would envy my friends who lived in town because the chores at the ranch pretty much stretched throughout the day. And they seemed to have more free time than I did." She heard him close his book; he took hers from her hands and put them both back on the floor. "But then I had unlimited access to horses and plenty of places to ride."

"That must have been nice."

"It still is...especially when the weather's nice. Do you ride?"

"I rode a few times as a teenager, but never enough to get the hang of it."

"If you have time during your visit, you could come out to the ranch, and we could take a short ride."

He wanted to see her again after they left here! Patrice smiled, excited by the prospect of not having everything end when they'd gone back to their separate lives.

Then the voice of common sense reminded her that an agreement to go riding didn't mean he was interested in a relationship. And what was she thinking anyway? She was barely out of one disastrous relationship, it was crazy to be thinking of jumping right into another.

The flames flickered and popped behind the screen. She jumped.

Stone chuckled. "Not getting used to that yet?"

"Most of the time I am. But occasionally it catches me off guard."

"What were you so busy thinking about?"

How would he react if she confessed that she'd been thinking about him? "Not thinking exactly, daydreaming mostly."

"About what?"

She shrugged. "This and that."

He turned her around so they lay face-to-face. Looking up at him, she smiled. Following the urging of his hands on her back, she leaned forward to kiss him.

A soft moan escaped her at the pleasure of having his mouth over hers once again. Such exquisite kisses...

His hands began caressing her, adding to the sensuality of the moment. Following his lead, she began moving her hands over him as well, marveling again at his hard strength.

A deep growl rumbled in his chest and then he was standing, sweeping her into his arms. He headed toward the bunk.

"Um, Stone? I thought we'd decided to wait."

"We *are* going to wait before making love, but there are other ways of loving, other ways to soothe the aching for a while."

When they reached the bunk, he lay her on the top one with her legs dangling over the side. He tucked the pillow under her head, took off her shoes, then moved his hands to the task of undoing her blue jeans. A shiver worked its way through her as he slowly drew the jeans down, taking the thermals and her panties with them.

He parted her knees, placing one leg on either side of him. Patrice's breath caught in her throat when he kissed her inner thigh and started working his way upward. The deliberate touch of his lips and the gentle brush of his beard were a killer combination. When he reached the center, he opened his mouth over her, teasing with his tongue and almost sending her straight over the edge.

Patrice grabbed fistfuls of her flannel shirt, holding on with a sense of desperation as if the fabric were her only link to the real world. The flannel was real, while the heat of Stone's mouth and the erotic sensations he was creating in her were part of a sweet dream, one she hoped she never awoke from.

She felt the powerful buildup of tension in her lower body and knew that if he kept it up, she was going to explode into a million pieces.

"Stone, maybe you should stop."

He lifted his head and looked at her. "You don't like it?"

"Oh, I like it...but I like it too much. I'm, um..."

"Getting close?"

She caught her bottom lip between her teeth and nodded.

He smiled. "Go ahead, darlin', take it over the top."

When he went back to where he'd left off, Patrice sighed. Her eyes drifted shut as sighs turned into soft moans, which in turn became cries signaling her release. Stone gradually slowed his movements, until he pulled back and placed whisper-soft kisses along the inside of her thigh again.

Her hands loosened their grip on her shirt, and the frantic beating of her heart settled to a more normal pace.

She opened her eyes to find Stone looking at her. He smiled, and she smiled back. The only word Patrice could think of was *wow*. She wasn't sure that would qualify as intelligent conversation so she didn't say anything.

Stone took a step closer, sliding his hands along the sides of her body until they rested at her waist. She wrapped her hands around his. After placing a kiss below her navel, he rested his head on her abdomen.

It would be so easy to drift off to sleep this way. But her sense of fair play wouldn't let her. Stone had given to her and asked nothing for himself. She wasn't sure how to give him the complete pleasure he'd given her, but she was going to try, certain he'd help her learn.

Releasing his hands, she ran her own through his hair. She felt the rush of blood to her cheeks even before she spoke. "I don't know much about this kind of thing, but is there something I could do for you?''

He lifted his head and looked at her. ''Only if you want to.''

''I wouldn't have offered otherwise. I'll need a little coaching, though.''

His smile was crooked and the light in his eyes wicked. ''I can do that.''

He helped her into a sitting position and then lifted her from the bunk. Together they removed the rest of their clothing, revealing to Patrice that her assumption that Stone was aroused was true.

He opened his sleeping bag in the bottom bunk. They both lay down, lying side by side. Stone gathered her into his arms, holding her close. She scooted up to kiss him. While they kissed, Stone took one of her hands in his and slowly lowered it down his body until it rested over his manhood. She closed her fingers around him.

At first he told her what felt good, but then the sharp intakes of his breath, his deep growls and the tremors throughout his body signaled his pleasure to her. She placed a soft kiss on his chest and inch by inch worked her way downward until her mouth and tongue could join her hands in touching him.

She might be a novice, but apparently she was a quick study, because in no time at all she sent Stone over the edge of his control. As he had done with her, she gradually slowed her motions until he lay still.

He reached down and pulled her up to lie by his side, holding her in his arms. Patrice wrapped the sleeping bag over them and nuzzled close to him.

"Sleepy?" Stone asked.

"Not really, since I had a nap this afternoon. Are you?"

"No."

She rested her hands on his chest, her chin on her hands and smiled at him. "Tell me more about being a cowboy."

He talked about the horses, the cattle, the roundups and the wide-open spaces. They moved on to talk about the books they were both reading at the moment and books in general. Books led to a discussion of favorite movies, movie sound tracks led to music.

"You like Vivaldi?" she asked in surprise.

He quirked one dark brow. "Sure. You didn't think I only listened to country and western music, did you?"

"Well, no, but I wouldn't have guessed classical."

He smiled mischievously. "Hey, I'm a well-rounded guy."

"Someone can be well-rounded and not listen to classical music."

"You're right."

"Can I have that in writing?"

With his finger, he drew letters over her back. "Patrice is right...exclamation point."

The exclamation point ran down the middle of her spine, the point landing on her lower back. He flashed her a devilish grin. She chuckled and then yawned.

"I think I'll turn off the lanterns for the night," he said.

She scooted to the side, moving her weight off him so he could get up. Stone added a few more logs to the fire and the stove and turned off the lanterns. Patrice watched in awe as once again he seemed to be such an integral part of the setting, even without his clothing. Obviously it wasn't the cowboy gear or hat that made him seem so at home, but the man himself.

He retrieved the other sleeping bag from the top bunk before lying down beside her and spreading it over them.

Patrice slid into his embrace. In a tangle of arms and legs, they curled around each other. They talked awhile longer, then she felt the urge to sleep nudging the edges of her mind.

She felt the brush of Stone's lips over hers and heard him say, "Sweet dreams, darlin'."

For the first time since arriving at the cabin, the scent of morning coffee was not in the air when she awoke. She smiled when she realized why. Stone wasn't up yet. He was there in the bunk, holding her close.

She noticed something else. The sound of the wind howling past the cabin walls. Was the storm starting again? Part of her liked the idea…well, actually, all of her liked the idea of prolonging their time here.

Stone shifted and she turned to look at him.

He smiled. "Good mornin'."

"Good morning."

Leaning forward, he kissed her. "Did you sleep well?"

"Very well. I stayed nice and warm."

He nuzzled her neck. "Me, too. And if I don't get up, it's going to get much warmer. Hot, even."

They kissed again. Patrice felt as though the sun had just risen in her soul. The intensity of it bordered on frightening.

Stone rolled onto his back, taking her with him, laying her over his chest. "Did I say good mornin'?"

"Yes, I think you did."

"Let me change that to great mornin'."

She laughed at the teasing light in his eye. But she definitely agreed that it was a great morning. The first morning she'd ever woken in a man's arms, and it had been wonderful. Of course, part of the appeal was the particular man she'd woken up to. Oh, heck, who was she kidding…it was *all* of the appeal.

It was hard to believe that in such a short time, this man had gotten through all her defenses, into her heart and her thoughts. Then again while it was only a matter of days it was a number of hours—twenty-four for each full day, minus the time they slept. In a more traditional relationship it would be weeks before a couple had spent that much time together.

Even so, was it long enough for her to fall in love?

Making love hadn't brought her any answers, only made her more desperate for them and added extra questions.

They lay snuggled together, kissing and whispering. They shared memories of past times, schools and places they'd traveled. When she mentioned the wind outside, he told her it might be the Chinook arriving. The hungry rumble of Stone's stomach finally rousted them from the bunk. They had breakfast, did the morning chores and then found themselves back in each other's arms on the couch.

The wind continued to howl all day. And when she was out in it, it didn't feel like a warm Chinook wind. It felt mighty cold to her. But by late afternoon when Patrice looked out the window, she could see the drifts of snow had grown smaller.

Stone came to stand behind her. "If this keeps up, we'll be out of here by tomorrow afternoon."

She turned to look over her shoulder. "Really?" It was a struggle to force herself to smile, even as her heart sank knowing that their time together was shrinking rapidly.

"Most likely."

"It melts as quickly as it falls."

"Sometimes. Not always. And at this elevation there will still be a considerable amount left on the ground, but not too much to drive over."

"I always thought four-wheel-drive vehicles could drive over anything."

"They can get through a lot more than a regular vehicle, but they have their limits, too." He put his arm around her shoulder. "Do you feel like taking a walk?"

"A walk would be nice, but it's awfully windy and while it is melting the snow, it doesn't feel very warm to me."

He chuckled. "No, I guess it doesn't at that."

"Maybe if it slows down later."

She turned and looked out the window. The trees were bending and their branches scattered their burdens of snow to the ground. Near the forest's edge, it almost looked as though it was snowing again.

"I guess I should finish the book I started if we're leaving soon," Patrice said.

"Feel free to take it with you if you don't get it done."

"All right. But if I can finish it, I won't have to."

"We, um, still have a condom."

She turned and looked up at him. "But we have a long night ahead of us."

He nodded. "You're right. Okay, let's read, but why don't you sit on my lap while we do?"

"All right."

They curled up together on the couch as they had the day before. Patrice found it hard to concentrate. She was too aware of the man holding her. When he started running his hand up and down her arm, she knew she'd never get anywhere near finishing the page she was on, let alone the whole book.

Leaning her head back, she looked up at him. "Stone."

"That condom is burnin' a hole in my pocket, darlin'."

Eight

Patrice laughed. "I've been trying not to think about it."

"I have, too. But it's a losing game for me." Stone flashed her a sexy smile. "So, what do you say?"

"I guess it's almost nighttime."

"Yes, the sun will be going down in about an hour."

"Would you like to have dinner first?"

He shook his head. "I'm not hungry for dinner. Are you?"

"No," she admitted. But she was hungry for the taste and feel of his lovemaking.

He sat up straighter on the couch, lifting her around until she straddled his lap. She wrapped her arms behind his neck, linking her fingers together. Leaning forward, she moved her mouth onto his. He pulled her closer, kissing her back with all the passion she'd come to expect from him. With his hands on her hips he aligned their lower bodies, making his need for her clear. Rocking against him caused them both to catch their breaths.

Stone whispered her name against her lips. When he pushed his hips forward, she gasped. The gasp faded to a sigh when he teased the inner edge of her lips, across the roof of her mouth and finally met her tongue again in a hungry welcome.

The sweet anticipation of things to come turned into a pulsing ache where he pressed against her. Instinctively she rocked her hips, setting off a chorus of soft sounds that were swallowed by their kiss.

Together, between kisses, they managed to bare each other to the waist. Stone trailed kisses from her lips to an already aroused nipple. Flattening her palms on his chest, Patrice teased both of his with her fingertips. When he grazed the edges of his teeth over her, her body arched. He moved his hands to the center of her back to keep her from falling off his lap. With his thumbs he stroked up and down her spine, sending shivers racing along its length.

"You are so responsive, darlin'."

"Is that a good thing?" Her voice was breathy and trembled when she spoke.

"A very good thing. Most men only fantasize about making love to a woman like you."

She felt the warmth of a blush on her cheeks. His words pleased her, but she doubted any other man's touch would affect her the same way—at least not at this point in her life. Maybe never again. Maybe Stone was her once-in-a-lifetime love. A love she would never be able to match, no matter how long she looked or how hard she tried.

And this might be the last time they made love.

Unless they got together after their return to civilization. Of course it wasn't wise to let her hopes wander too far in that direction. Not if she wanted to enjoy tonight the way she needed to…to the fullest extent possible.

He pulled her body to his and coaxed her into bringing their mouths together. She ran her tongue across his full bottom lip until he opened to her and invited her in. How could she do anything other than accept his offer?

By the time they pulled away, they were both breathing raggedly and rapidly. The quivering ache deep within Patrice had increased a hundredfold. Looking into Stone's clear blue eyes, the words "I love you" were on the tip of her tongue. They wanted to tumble out, but she wasn't sure how he would take them. He hadn't said anything like them to her, hadn't committed himself emotionally in any way.

In his eyes, she could read want and desire, but love? She didn't think so. Once again she wondered if he still loved his wife.

He threaded his hands through her hair. "Shall we go to bed, while I can still walk there?"

She nodded. "Yes, please."

Placing his hands around her waist, he helped her off his lap. After adjusting his blue jeans, he stood. Taking her hand, he walked to the bunk. Both sleeping bags were still on the bottom one.

He helped her with the rest of her clothes and she helped him with his. Pulling the condom from the pocket of his jeans, he slipped it beneath one of the pillows.

Standing full height again, he reached out and took her face between his hands. Placing hers on his chest, she moved her fingers until the crisp dark hair curled around them and tickled her palms. She leaned forward and kissed the warm skin over his heart. A shudder surged through his muscles.

She smiled as she felt the response echo through his whole body, including the hot length of him pressed against her belly. He kissed her forehead and drew her with him onto the bottom bunk.

He took his time, loving her leisurely and loving her well. Only when she was beginning to suspect she couldn't take anymore without exploding into a million pieces did he retrieve the foil packet, slip on the condom and position himself between her legs. Slowly, inch by inch, he joined them together.

A half gasp, half moan escaped her throat.

"I know, darlin'. I know. So sweet."

A nod of agreement was all she could manage. Forming words was completely out of the question.

Pulling back, then pushing forward again, he began the rhythmic motions that would propel them to completion. She mirrored his actions. Gradually he increased the tempo and the strength of his movements.

Patrice felt herself slipping away, existing only in the intense sensations building within her and the sounds of intimacy coming from her and being answered by Stone.

She tried to hang on to the feeling of euphoria, never wanting to leave this place of awareness. But when he tensed and started to shudder against her, she lost control. Holding him tightly and tilting her hips upward, she felt the sensations build the last critical fraction that sent her tumbling after him.

He collapsed over her, burying his head against her breasts. It took all her remaining strength to lift her arms so she could run her fingers through his hair. He nuzzled against her, his beard tickling her sensitized flesh.

Moving her hands lower, she skimmed them over the hard planes of his back and shoulders. With a deep groan, he rolled onto his back, pulling her on top of him. Sighing, she relaxed and rested her cheek on his chest.

He took a deep breath and let it out in a whistle. "It keeps getting better and better. If this is cabin fever, I hope it never goes away."

A flash of joy sparked in her. Was there the hint of a future for them in his words? Did he mean it was better and better for them as a couple? Or was he speaking only of himself?

As they lay in each other's arms, she waited for him to turn the conversation in that direction again, but he didn't. Once the heat of their lovemaking left their bodies, Stone pulled the other sleeping bag over them.

He seemed in no hurry to sleep, holding and caressing her. Most of the night was spent sharing kisses and gazing into each other's eyes.

Patrice didn't remember falling asleep. But she felt herself coming through the stages of waking, so she must have. Sometime during the night, she'd slipped down to lie at Stone's side. He had one arm around her, holding her close. One of her hands rested over his, the other was on his waist.

She shut her eyes again, absorbing all the details of him. Against her better judgment, she let her thoughts drift to how wonderful it would be to have every morning start this way.

A beautiful dream, Patrice, but don't get used to the idea.

But it was such a tempting dream. One she longed to fall into and not awaken from. Beneath her closed eyelids, she felt moisture building. She didn't dare let Stone catch her crying. He'd want to know why. And she might find herself blurting out her love for him.

That wasn't the way she wanted him to remember her. She wanted him to have memories of their days together as fun and passion-filled. No way did she want to be remembered as poor Patrice who turned knock-your-socks-off lovemaking into a declaration of love. At least there was something she could do to prevent that from happening.

Slowly and carefully, she slipped from the bunk, tucked the sleeping bag around Stone and dressed in her abandoned clothes. After adding logs to the fires, she started the coffee and breakfast preparations.

Everything was just about ready when she felt a sense of Stone's watching her. Looking over her shoulder, she saw that he *was* awake and watching.

She smiled at him. "Good morning."

"Mornin'."

Her smile grew bigger. She loved the sound of his voice. But right after he woke up, it had a roughness that thrilled her even more.

She walked to the bunk. "Breakfast is almost ready."

He stretched and sat up, the sleeping bag slipping down to his waist, leaving his bare chest revealed to her gaze. She tried not to stare, but it was such a temptation. Staring left her wanting to touch. Touching would lead to places they couldn't go now even if they wanted to.

Stone rubbed his hand over his beard. "I guess I'd better get up then."

He started scooting toward the edge of the bunk. Patrice quickly turned and walked back to the kitchen area to check everything. She kept her back to him until she heard the sound of a zipper. Turning, she watched him pull on his thermal top and slip into his shirt.

He looked up and smiled at her. "All ready?"

Her heart skipped a beat. All ready for what, she wondered. "Ready?" Her voice was quiet.

"Breakfast?"

"Oh, of course." If he hadn't been watching, she would have smacked her forehead with the palm of her hand. What else could he have meant? It wasn't likely that he would get all dressed and then suggest any kind of lovemaking. The warmth of a blush heated her cheeks.

He walked to the table and sat down. She poured the coffee and served the oatmeal and canned peaches.

Stone ate in silence for a while, then said, "Before we go, we'll need to fill out an inventory slip so Mack can see to restocking the line shack."

"I would imagine that especially during the winter it's important to keep a full cupboard."

"Yes, it is."

They talked of neutral topics after that, but the upcoming departure was now well and truly front and center in Patrice's thoughts. Just the cleaning up, the inventory and a quick check of the path down and they would be on their way back to their own lives.

Silence filled the room. They went about the breakfast cleanup. They rolled up the sleeping bags, putting them and the pillows back into the cupboard. Stone took a clipboard with a stack of inventory sheets and a pencil off the bottom shelf. Patrice read off the items. Stone counted what was there and gave her the numbers.

Working together it took little time to get through the list. When it was finished, he folded it and put it into his wallet.

"I'm going to check out the road," he said.

"All right."

When he headed off, Patrice followed, making the trip out back. She returned to the cabin before Stone did. Looking around the room, moments from the last week flashed through her memory...some made her smile, others made her catch her breath.

But their total effect on her now was to make her eyes fill with tears. At times it had felt as though they'd been here forever, but now it felt as though they'd just arrived. She gathered the clothes she'd been wearing when her car had driven off the road and stacked them on one of the benches.

The door opened. She swiftly dried her tears and turned to face Stone. "How does the road look?"

"Good at this end. I called Mack and he says that the highway down below has been plowed and is clear all the way to town."

She forced a smile. "That's good news."

"Yes. I guess we need to put out the fires and head out."

He took care of the stove first. On his way to the fireplace, he picked up the books from beside the couch. "Did you want to take this with you?"

She walked over to him, taking the book from his hand, pressing it to her chest. "Yes, I would. Thank you."

He nodded. "No problem."

She expected him to turn toward the fireplace. Instead he continued to look at her.

"Ah, hell, darlin'," he said, reaching for her.

She set the book on the back of the couch and stepped into his open arms. Going up on tiptoe, she met his lips in a hungry kiss. A kiss that quickly raged out of control.

Before she realized what was happening, she

found herself lying in front of the fireplace with Stone's sheepskin-lined jacket under her head, the smooth wood floor, warm from the fire, against her back.

From inside a sensual haze, she realized he was undressing her and then himself. She raised her arms toward him. He smiled as he lowered himself into them. Wrapped in each other's arms, they kissed again...and again.

There was nothing on her mind other than the incredible feelings racing through her body and the awareness of this man in her arms and in her heart.

She parted her legs to let him closer. He moved down and forward, joining them together. With a sigh, she closed her eyes, letting her hands roam over his back. She could feel his muscles tensing and relaxing as he moved. Matching her pace to his, she rocked against him.

Their loving wasn't as gentle as it had been last night, there was a desperate edge to it. Patrice tried to analyze why, but the sensations were increasing at a rapid rate and she couldn't seem to focus on anything except the approaching moment of bliss.

As she reached the edge, Stone drove deeply several more times and followed her, murmuring incoherent words against her neck. His lips and breath hot on her skin.

She floated in the security of his arms. So happy

that they'd gotten to make love one more time before leaving.

An icy chill swept through her. "*Ohmigod!*
Stone, what have we done?"

Nine

Stone gazed down at her, a peaceful look of love-drugged satisfaction on his face.

He repeated her question. "What have we done?" After blinking several times, a pained look settled over his features. He swore as he sat up. Lifting her into his arms, he gathered her close. "I'm sorry, Patrice."

She rested her head on his shoulder. "Me, too."

"Damn, what came over me? I know better than to make love without protection. What in the hell was I thinking?"

"It's not all your fault. I could have stopped you, but I...it didn't even enter my mind that the condoms were gone until afterward."

"I know the feeling, darlin'. I didn't even think about it afterward."

She glanced at her stomach. How likely was it that Stone's baby would begin and grow there?

It's too early for you to panic, Patrice.

There would be plenty of time for that once she knew one way or the other. Then she would have to worry about what to do.

She sat up straighter. "I guess we should be getting ready to go."

Stone tightened his arms around her. "Don't you think we should discuss this?"

"Everything might be fine. Why worry now?"

"You might be pregnant."

"But I might not be," she said.

"We should look at our options in case you are."

She took a deep breath and released it on a sigh. "Why not wait until we know?"

"If we have a plan in place, we won't be caught completely off guard if there should be a baby."

"And if there's not a baby, we'll have wasted all that time planning."

She was startled when she heard her words. She was usually the first one to start planning far in advance, making endless lists. Always having a contingency plan and a backup for the contingency plan. Only her spur-of-the-moment trip to Montana hadn't been considered in detail.

Maybe that was going to be the new style of her life.

She wriggled out of Stone's lap, then stood and went to gather her clothes. His mouth set in a grim line, Stone also dressed.

"I want you to know that I'll be there for you throughout this."

Part of her was grateful for his words, but another part that wanted him to declare his love rather than his intent to help was angry.

"There may not be a *this* for you to worry about," she snapped.

He turned, his eyes narrowed, his hands on his hips. "Getting angry isn't going to help."

"Oh, pardon me, Mr. Garrett. I'm not getting angry. I'm already angry."

"I said I was sorry."

A throbbing was beginning behind her temples. "Yes, and I told you it wasn't only your fault. I'm not angry about what happened, just your attitude about it."

"My attitude? I'm offering to help. Would you be happier if I simply abandoned you? Left you to handle everything on your own?"

"I'm perfectly capable of doing just that."

Sure, Patrice. You just lost your business. How are you going to take care of a baby and rebuild your life at the same time?

But there might not be a baby…she had to keep

sight of that fact. And she had to be sure Stone kept sight of it, too.

"Fine then. Be that way," he said.

"That way? What does that mean exactly?"

"All-fired, independent Ms. City Girl. But know this, if there is a baby I have rights, too. And you can be damned sure I'll do what I can to get them."

"Is that a threat?"

"No, darlin'. That's a pledge on the name of Garrett. Ask around while you're in Clancy. You'll learn how much weight it holds in these parts."

He turned his back and went to the fireplace to put out the fire. She wondered if he was putting out the passionate fire within himself, too.

Patrice gathered her own clothes and the book she was borrowing. Without another word to Stone, she carried them to the truck, laying them on the passenger seat.

"Stubborn, macho cowboy," she mumbled under her breath.

A half-dozen angry remarks had come to mind after his last statement, but she'd recognized the futility of arguing over a hypothetical situation.

Instead of going into the cabin, she chose to wait on the front porch for him to finish inside. Besides not wanting to continue their argument, she didn't need to see the room empty nor to look again at the places where they'd made love. Although their times together were beautiful memories, it didn't seem wise to be reminded of them after what had just happened.

Their final lovemaking had been heavenly...but with a bittersweet ending when she considered the possible consequences of their actions.

Stone came out carrying his rifle. He shut the door, shaking it to be sure it was secure. Then he checked the shutters across the front of the cabin. With long strides that quickly took him across the yard, he reached the truck, hooked the rifle on the rack and started the engine.

Patrice took a last look around the meadow and followed his path.

Stone glanced over at Patrice. She pressed against the passenger door as tightly as she had on their drive to the cabin. Part of him wanted to apologize. Take back the angry words and make peace between them. But another part felt it was best to leave things as they were. After the way he'd lost control of the situation and made love to her, keeping his distance was wisest.

Val was the only other woman he'd ever made love to without a condom. So his forgetting was strange and unsettling.

Thoughts of Val drifted into an area he rarely let himself think about—the baby she'd been carrying. The baby he'd talked her into conceiving. And now look what he'd done. That Patrice would find herself pregnant was not guaranteed, but it was a possibility. A possibility which he should never have allowed to develop.

A possibility he had to hope and pray didn't come to be.

Nevertheless, he found his mind considering what they would do if she was carrying his child. She didn't seem like the type to simply hand the baby over to him and go on with her life. And he wasn't sure that's what he would want, either.

Would she marry him?

Time out, Garrett. You don't even know if there's going to be a baby.

That was what had started them arguing. He really should have held his remarks. Right then hadn't been the best time to discuss the matter. It had made Patrice defensive and edgy. Not at all the sweet, even-tempered woman she'd been throughout their stay.

Despite having seen this new side of her, he began to imagine what it would be like waking up with her in his arms every morning. More vivid in his mind was the experience of falling to sleep after making love to her. He'd done both and wouldn't mind repeating either one. But on a daily basis for the rest of his life? He wasn't sure.

Besides, would they have a chance for a lasting relationship if they got married when they didn't love each other? Would their child realize there wasn't love between them?

He did *like* her, enjoyed being around her and delighted in their lovemaking. But was that enough to build a future on?

Patrice was grateful to see the sign announcing their arrival in Clancy. The ride into town had been made in awkward silence. Stone turned the truck into Bob's Garage, just past the first intersection. She understood why when she spotted her car in one of the service bays.

Stone turned off the engine. "Let's get your things."

She nodded, opened her door and hopped out. First, Stone introduced her to Bob. Next, they went to her car and took her personal belongings from inside and from the trunk. The small items she took into the cab. Stone lifted the suitcase into the truck bed.

Silence took over again as they made the drive through town and out to her grandmother's house. Stone pulled into the driveway. Within moments, the front door flew open and Dorothy Winston stepped onto the porch. Patrice quickly headed toward her.

Grandma opened her arms. "Patty, honey! What a surprise!"

She hugged the petite older woman. Immediately

a sense of peace settled into her heart and frazzled nerves. "Hi, Grandma. Think you can put up with some company?"

Dorothy took Patrice's face between her hands. "If it's you, definitely."

The sound of footsteps coming up the wooden stairs announced Stone's arrival. He carried her suitcase in one hand, her laptop and briefcase in the other.

Her grandmother released her from the hug, but kept an arm around her. "Stone Garrett, as I live and breathe. How are you doing?"

"Just fine, ma'am. How have you been?"

"It doesn't matter how I've been. At the moment, I'm in seventh heaven."

Stone nodded at the suitcase. "Would you like me to take this upstairs?"

"Please," Dorothy answered. "Second bedroom on the right."

Once he headed into the house, Patrice said, "I have a few other things in the cab. Let me get them."

Grandma walked to the truck with her, chatting away about how good it was to see her, but what a surprise. Stone was coming down the stairs as they walked in the front door. His eyes met Patrice's across the distance.

"Stone," her grandmother said. "Would you

like to stay for an early dinner? I can have it ready in half an hour.''

''Thanks for the offer, but I really need to be getting back to the ranch.''

''Did you have much damage from the storm?''

''Mack says it's not too bad.''

''You've been away from home then?''

Patrice spoke up. ''I'll explain it all, Grandma. Let me walk Mr. Garrett to his truck.''

''All right. I'll put on some water for tea. Nice seeing you again, Stone. Don't be such a stranger around here.''

Stone and Patrice walked side by side. When they reached the end of the walkway, she stopped. He came to a halt a few steps later and turned to face her.

''Thanks again for coming to my rescue,'' she said.

''Glad I could help.''

She looked down and then back to Stone. ''Drive carefully.''

''I will.'' He tucked his hands into his jacket pockets. ''Enjoy your visit with your grandmother.''

''I will.''

She waited a few seconds for him to say something else, but he only nodded to her and walked around to the driver's side of the truck. Retracing their path, she headed toward the house. They waved briefly when he pulled out of the driveway.

Patrice stood on her grandmother's porch, watching until the taillights of his truck faded in the distance. A great empty hole opened in the region of her heart.

He was gone. He'd been part of her every waking moment, and many of her sleeping ones for days now…and suddenly he was gone.…

She felt moisture gather in the corners of her eyes.

How did he feel about leaving her? Was he relieved? Because they'd argued, or would he have been relieved to get rid of her anyway? Just because they'd made love didn't mean he felt any regrets about their separating.

Watching him drive off was killing her. The peace and quiet she'd found at the cabin and in his arms slowly seeped from her soul. Closing her eyes, she tried to compose herself. She didn't want Grandma to see her crying. Tears would prompt questions, and she didn't have any logical answers.

She reminded herself that while at the cabin, he'd mentioned her coming out to the ranch to ride. But he hadn't repeated the invitation. Had he changed his mind about wanting her to visit? Was it only something he'd said in passing, never planning to follow up on? Or was it their argument that had made him change his mind…or had the events of this afternoon simply driven that notion from his mind?

After wiping the tears away, she opened the front door and walked into the house.

Stone watched Patrice in his rearview mirror until he could no longer see her.

When their time together had begun, he had looked forward to this moment—dropping her off safely and going back to his own life. Now that the moment had come, he was confused by mixed feelings.

Deep inside, he suspected he was going to miss her. Hell, who was he kidding? He missed her already.

No, the logical side of him argued, he'd gotten used to having her around...that was all. Once he got back into the routine at the ranch, he would forget all about her.

Images from the days past floated through his mind. Her sweet smile first thing in the morning, the sound of her laughter and the sexy moans and cries she made while making love.

Whoa, pardner, don't start thinking about that.

The last thing he needed to be pondering was the physical side of their time together or he'd have to hit a cold shower as soon as he got home.

Throughout the rest of the day, after conferring with Mack about the ranch and Virginia about the house, playing fetch the stick with Elwood and walking the main compound; his mind strayed to Patrice. He wondered what she was doing and whether she might be thinking of him, too.

Sitting in his office after dinner, the thoughts finally got the best of him. He grabbed the local phone directory and looked up the number for Dorothy Winston.

As he listened to the sound of ringing in the receiver, his gaze drifted to the mantel and the framed wedding photograph.

The realization landed on him like a ton of bricks...he hadn't thought about Val since he'd arrived home.

He wasn't sure if he should feel pleased about that or guilty. Val had been the love of his life. From the moment she'd walked into their twelfth-grade homeroom, his heart had been hers. It had been love at first sight and he'd fallen hard.

"Hello." The sound of someone answering the phone snapped Stone back to the present.

"Mrs. Winston, this is Stone Garrett. Could I speak to Patrice?"

"Well, of course. And thank you for taking such good care of my granddaughter."

He almost said, my pleasure, but caught himself in time. Since the remark would have been true in more ways than one, he felt it was best to avoid it. "Glad to be of assistance, ma'am."

* * *

Patrice had spent the late afternoon pouring out the troubles she'd had with Neil to her grandmother. In turn she received the sympathy and understanding she'd been needing when she'd started this way. Unfortunately, at the moment, there was another troubled place in her heart, one she didn't dare mention to Grandma.

She was surprised when the older woman called her to the phone. Only the man at the garage, and of course Stone knew she was here. It was too late for the garage to be open, and she sincerely doubted Stone would be calling.

He'd been first and foremost in her thoughts since she'd gotten here. Even though she was thrilled to be with her grandmother, he was an ever constant presence.

Maybe it was because they'd spent so much time together in close quarters. The forced intimacy might have created whatever strange bond was now connecting them. Being away, it almost felt as though she was having withdrawals. She kept remembering snippets of conversations, the touch of his hands on her body, the feel of him sinking into her.

"Hello," she said into the phone.

"Hello, Patrice."

"Stone."

"I, um, just thought I'd call to see how you were doing."

"I'm fine." It was only partly a lie; she actually was feeling better now that she was talking to him.

"It feels odd not being with you tonight."

She chuckled. "Yes, it does, doesn't it?"

"I miss you, darlin'." His voice was low and intimate.

She glanced through the dining room, into the kitchen to be sure her grandmother was there and busy before she answered. "I miss you, too."

"I'm sorry about our argument today. I was out of line."

He was apologizing. Although he couldn't see her through the phone, she smiled. "I'm sorry, too."

"The whole incident caught me off guard and I overreacted."

"We both did. Besides that…" She wrapped the phone cord around her finger. "When it got closer to leaving time, I realized I was going to miss the cabin."

"Even the lack of plumbing?"

She chuckled. "Not that so much as the peacefulness and the beauty of the surroundings."

Her grandmother walked into the room. "Invite him for dinner tomorrow night, Patty."

"Stone, Grandma wants to know if you can join us for dinner tomorrow night?"

"All right. I'd like that."

She nodded to her grandmother, who gave her a thumbs-up sign.

"Grandma? What time?"

"Six."

"How's six?" she asked Stone.

"Six is fine."

She looked toward her grandmother. "All right. Six it is then."

Grandma smiled and headed toward the stairs.

Patrice made a mental note to get the clothes she'd borrowed at the line shack washed and ready to return before then, too. Of course if she didn't that would provide her with a reason to go to his ranch…giving her another chance to see him.

But did she really want to keep seeing him? The answer depended on whether or not she was expecting. And on figuring out what Stone had meant when he'd said he would fight for his rights to a child. Had that been anger talking? And when he said he would be there for her throughout, had he meant financially, emotionally or both?

She didn't know—and she wasn't sure which she hoped he'd meant, either. That was most troubling of all, not knowing her own mind. Not understanding someone else was one thing, but not understanding yourself was another.

So much of what she'd said and done recently was not like her at all.

Especially the way she'd fallen in love and into Stone's arms so easily. With the hurt and pain of Neil's betrayal so fresh in her mind and heart, she would have thought that it would be months before she'd look at another man.

But she'd done more than look at Stone...

What, if anything, was going to happen with their relationship now?

Ten

Patrice was a bundle of nerves by the time six the next evening rolled around. She dressed in a wool skirt and knitted sweater that she'd bought for a fall business trip to Chicago. It was smart, stylish and comfortable.

She took extra time with her makeup. After spending so many days without, putting it on felt strange. She set her hair on hot rollers, making it fall in soft waves rather than lying straight and flat.

At least physically she was ready for the evening ahead. If she could only get the emotions whipped into shape. She headed for the kitchen to see if there was anything she could help with.

Her grandmother was stirring a steaming pot on the stove. "Well, don't you look nice. Turn around."

Patrice made a slow circle.

"Good, no slip hanging down."

Patrice smiled. Grandma always checked for hanging slips whenever they were together. "Is there anything I can help with?"

"Why don't you go into the dining room and set the table?"

"All right."

"And be sure to listen for the doorbell."

As if her ears hadn't been tuned to that exact pitch for the last hour. "I will."

Everything she needed was in the china cabinet and in no time she had the table set for three.

She was about to head back to the kitchen when the doorbell rang. Nibbling on her bottom lip and smoothing her skirt, she walked to the front hallway. With her hand on the doorknob, she took a deep breath and let it out slowly.

She opened the door and smiled at Stone. Her heart tripped over a beat at the sight of him. "You're right on time."

His gaze swept her from head to toe. An unsettled feeling began in the pit of her stomach. It wasn't the heated gaze she was used to getting from him. It was cool and impersonal.

He removed his cowboy hat. "Evenin', Patrice."

"Hello, Stone." She pushed open the screen door and stepped back. "Come in."

Standing in the hallway, he handed her his hat and jacket. She hung them on the coatrack beside the door.

"How have you been?" she asked.

"Fine. You?"

An answer and another question for her in two words…hard to believe they'd talked together for hours. She'd expected to be greeted with open arms and his withdrawal put her on the defensive, keeping her from making any overt approaches toward him.

The same awkwardness carried over to dinner and lingered through coffee. If her grandmother hadn't been there to keep the conversation moving, Patrice didn't think they would be talking at all.

Despite his verbal reticence, every now and then Patrice would glance up and catch Stone watching her, usually with coolness. Once when she'd been laughing she caught a different look on his face— one that almost looked like pain.

Even more distressing was how he left as soon as he could after the meal without appearing impolite.

"Thank you for dinner, Mrs. Winston."

"Must you go so soon?" Dorothy asked.

"Some repair supplies we've been waiting for

arrived late this afternoon and we need to get an early start in the morning.''

"Let me put together a plate of leftovers to take home with you for a snack," Dorothy said.

"That's not necessary," Stone answered. But before he'd finished, the older woman was halfway to the kitchen. Once they were alone, he reached into his back pocket, pulled out his wallet and took out a business card.

He handed it to Patrice. "If you need to contact me in a few weeks' time, here's where I can be reached."

She wanted to demand that he tell her why his warm apologetic behavior on the phone last night had changed so drastically. And how he could calmly present her with his card when the matter she might have to contact him about was the possible existence of their child. She could have accepted this attitude from the cold, taciturn cowboy who'd picked her up along the side of the road. But not from the tender, caring man who'd smiled, laughed and made love to her so sweetly.

She tucked the card into the pocket of her skirt. "Thanks."

"If you're in Phoenix, feel free to call collect."

Only her grandmother's arrival prevented her from letting her jaw drop or from giving him a piece of her mind. Instead she felt something twist and break inside her.

It seemed she'd done it again...fallen in love with the wrong man. And so soon after she'd discovered the first mistake. Lord, what was wrong with her?

Inside she felt as battered and bruised as she had when she'd loaded up her car and headed north.

Stone pushed the gas pedal to the floor when he reached the highway.

What were you thinkin', pardner?

The car, the clothes she'd been wearing when he'd rescued her...both had been dead giveaways to the differences between them. The woman was luxury cars, and he was pickup trucks. But he'd gotten used to the fresh-face beauty in the too-big clothes. Having the door open to the smooth, sophisticated woman she'd changed into overnight had been a major shock.

All his hopes for recapturing some of the magic that had been between them at the cabin had skidded like a pickup hitting black ice. And all his thoughts about the possibilities of the two of them getting together to raise their baby were laughable now that he reconsidered them.

It would never work, not in a thousand years. Hell, not in a million!

She had his card, hopefully she would call. If she didn't then he'd call her in a month or so to find out about the baby.

Suddenly a strong gut reaction gripped him. While there was no hope for him with Patrice, he saw a bright future for him and the child. Part-time or full-time father, whichever ended up being his role, he would give it his all.

Throughout the night images from their time at the cabin haunted him. Vivid images, including what it felt like to hold her, the effect of her smiles on his pulse rate and the trust in her eyes.

He also remembered the strong sense of anticipation he'd felt while waiting for six o'clock to roll around so he could see her again.

And then the time had come and he'd been standing on the porch, looking in at a stranger. The way she'd dressed for dinner—the clothes, the makeup, the hair were probably part of her daily life in Arizona. Most likely, she didn't realize how different they made her look from the woman he'd gotten to know.

As the sun rose over the new day, he decided that he wouldn't shut the door on Patrice so quickly. Somewhere behind the chilly facade was the warm, fun-loving woman he'd made love to.

He'd been wrong to shut himself off from her without exploring further.

Well, at the end of the day's chores, he'd head back into town and correct his mistake.

Patrice had hoped Stone would have a change of heart and call. But each day of her visit came and went with no word from him. She felt her spirits sinking.

She missed him. It felt as though some vital part of her was no longer there.

When she'd discovered Neil's deception it had left her hurting…it had broken her heart. But it seemed as though when Stone left, he had taken her heart with him…leaving her with an aching void.

Long into the nights, while her grandmother slept, she would cry quietly into her pillow. During the days she had half her attention keyed to hear the phone and the doorbell.

She finally called her parents in Phoenix. It didn't surprise her that they hadn't noticed she was out of town. Their paths rarely crossed these days. They were retired and heavily into their golf game. Her mother did agree to go over to her condo and water the potted plants—if they hadn't already died.

At the beginning of her second week in Montana, the arrival of her period slammed her mood even further to the ground. It didn't last long this month, which was unusual, but she figured it had to be the altitude and the stress she'd been under.

Overall she was relieved. It was going to be hard enough putting her life back together with only herself to think about…rebuilding and taking care of a baby would have been much more difficult.

Except a baby would have given her a part of

Stone. A tangible reminder of their time together and her love for him.

But would it be fair to the child to have to face the world with a single parent, just so she could hold on tighter to the memories? And what if Stone really did make good on his threats to fight for his rights? Did he intend to try for full custody? How would she survive losing her baby, too? When she didn't have a clue as to how she was going to survive losing the love of her life...

She glanced at his card several times a day, thinking about calling. But never did, not sure what to say. If he'd only given a small sign of encouragement the night he'd been there for dinner it would have been easier. As it was, she had to assume he was just a typical guy, taking advantage of free sex when it came his way.

Oh well, she really needed to turn her attention to putting her life back together.

She managed to put on a happy face for her grandmother. And she truly did enjoy their time together. It was as soothing as she'd known it would be. Her grandmother always had that effect on her. It was one of the constants in her life. Something that didn't change as the years slipped by.

A place where she knew she always had a refuge. How difficult it must be for people who didn't have anyone in their lives that meant so much to them.

She wondered about Stone. Whether he had anyone to turn to when life was being especially brutal.

She assumed his wife had served that role when they'd been together. But what about now?

And why should she worry and fret about him anyway? He obviously wasn't giving her a second thought.

Frowning, Stone leaned against the stack of hospital pillows. He was surprised his anger hadn't sent smoke out his ears, setting off the fire alarm. There was nothing he hated more than being laid up in a hospital bed. Especially when it was a hospital so far from home that they'd airlifted him there.

He looked at the clock, wondering when his next round of pain medication was due. It had better be soon, the throbbing in his knee was kicking in…big time. He'd injured it years ago playing college football, and it hadn't bothered him much since the surgery he'd had back then. But it was sure hurting now.

Running his hands through his hair, he groaned and silently cursed the ice patch he hadn't seen in time to avoid. He'd slipped and come down square on his knee.

Glancing at the nightstand, he glared at the phone. He would have to buzz the nurse to have her move it within reach. The traction kept him from doing much of anything without asking for assistance. That was almost enough to keep him from calling Patrice. But not quite. What stopped him was his need to be able to see her face while he talked.

He wanted to be able to gauge her reaction to his words. Wanted to see if there was a flash of the woman he knew in her eyes. There was no way he could get the whole picture from a phone conversation.

But he was going to be laid up several weeks. Could he afford to wait that long? Patrice would be on her way back to Phoenix before the doctor sprung him out of here.

He supposed he could fly to Arizona to see her. Or he could ask the nurse for the phone and call her now.

No, he really wanted to talk face-to-face. Only one choice then—he was just going to have to wait.

As the day she'd planned to leave for home grew closer, Patrice's mood dropped lower.

"Are you all right, Patty?" Dorothy asked over breakfast one morning.

"I'm going to leave soon. And I don't really want to."

"I thought you'd be happy to get back to Phoenix."

Patrice shrugged. "There might be a small number of my clients that I could recover, but during the time I was building the business and then while dating Neil, I lost touch with most of my friends. Mom and Dad are there of course, but I don't see much of them.''

Dorothy took a sip of her coffee. "Have you thought about settling somewhere else?"

"Not really."

"What about moving to Clancy?"

"Moving to Clancy?"

She hadn't thought about it, but now that she did, it made sense. In her time of distress, she had headed straight here—Montana and Grandma calling to her troubled mind. And other than the dilemma with Stone, her time here had been pleasant and healing.

Everyone she'd met in town was warm and friendly. And living in Clancy would mean she could see Grandma more frequently…every day if she wanted.

But were there enough people to build a bookkeeping business? Or should she try something else? Maybe open a shop of some kind? The wide-open spaces and gorgeous scenery were another thing in its favor.

"I'm going to have to build my life from scratch again. There's no reason I can't do that here just as well as in Phoenix."

Her grandmother smiled. "No reason at all, dear."

* * *

Patrice checked the weather conditions before making the trip to Phoenix. The road back through the mountains brought thoughts of Stone roaring into her mind.

In Arizona, she traded in her car for a used mini-truck with four-wheel drive. Some of her things she put into storage and arranged for the rest to be shipped to Montana.

When she contacted her client list to say good-bye, she was surprised to find many had been hoping she'd planned to reopen. Their loyalty touched her, but didn't alter her decision to move north.

She'd already accepted a part-time job in Clancy's yarn and hobby shop. Working with the customers and, much to her delight, taking care of the bookkeeping. Grandma had wanted her to share the house, but instead Patrice decided to rent a small apartment above the tack and feed store across Main Street from work. Having lived on her own since graduating from high school, she was used to her privacy and suspected her grandmother was, too.

On the return trip to Montana, she kept close tabs on the weather and road conditions ahead. She didn't dare take a chance of having to call Sheriff Jackson. Of course he might not send Stone to rescue her this time, but it was a chance she wasn't willing to risk.

She didn't have to worry too much about seeing Stone around town. From what she'd heard of his talk with Grandmother, it had been years since the two of them had crossed paths.

One of these days she was going to have to call and tell Stone she wasn't pregnant. Then again, she could wait and see how long he would go before calling her to ask.

Patrice settled right into her new job and apartment. She saw her grandmother every day, either at the house or in town. Everything seemed to be working out perfectly until she was at work one afternoon and was hit by a sudden rush of nausea.

It lasted several hours and then was gone as quickly as it had come. She didn't think anything more of it until it happened again the next day. And then the next...

By the fourth day, she was starting to get worried and made an appointment to see the doctor immediately.

Forty-five minutes later she walked out of his office with a stack of brochures and a prescription for prenatal vitamins in her purse.

Eleven

Patrice was so focused on the doctor's revelation that she completely forgot about the wedding she'd promised to attend with her grandmother that evening. She gave serious consideration to canceling, but Grandma sounded so excited about Patrice going with her that she didn't have the heart to change the plans.

Her afternoon nausea had disappeared, as usual, so she couldn't truthfully plead that she wasn't feeling well. The doctor had explained that what she was experiencing was morning sickness, which despite the name didn't always come in the morning. He'd also told her that it wasn't unheard of to have some light spotting after conception.

During her appointment she had been glad to hear that either circumstance didn't mean anything was wrong with the pregnancy. Once she got home, she began to face the fact that she was going to have a baby—Stone Garrett's baby.

She was going to have to call him soon. Tomorrow she had the day off from work, but she and Grandma had planned to do some exploring in the attic. Of course, the attic could wait. Besides, how long would the phone call take?

Once Stone knew, she would have to tell her grandmother, too…and her parents.

She sat on the couch, curling her legs and tucking them to the side. Her eyes filled with tears. Closing them, she rested her forehead on the armrest. In order to get through the bride and groom making their wedding vows without weeping buckets, she needed to let out some of the emotions building inside her.

Granting herself the luxury of a good long cry was something she had to do.

Patrice sat in the pew between her grandmother and the pastor's wife. The church was decorated with flowers and flickering candles. She couldn't help thinking about Neil and the wedding they'd been planning, as well as Stone and the wedding that would never be for them, either.

It was a struggle not to view tonight's festivities

with a cynical eye. But despite her run of bad luck, she still believed that somewhere in the world true love existed. She just wasn't sure if it would ever exist for her.

The organ began playing louder as the ushers escorted the bride and groom's families to their places. The music changed and the bridesmaids began down the aisle. The petite flower girl and small ring bearer followed.

The wedding march boomed from the choir loft as the bride and her father stepped into the doorway. Patrice stood with the rest of the guests and turned toward the back of the church. The bride looked radiant. It was impossible not to smile as they walked past.

Before Patrice turned to face the front again, a tall, dark-haired man caught her eye. Her first thought was that the man looked a lot like Stone would without his beard. Then his gaze met hers, and he nodded in her direction.

Quickly she turned, her hand moving instinctively to rest over her stomach.

Dear heavens! He's the last person I feel like dealing with tonight. But, oh, my…doesn't he look handsome without his beard?

He had a strong jawline and chin that didn't need the addition of a beard to enhance his features. But as she knew, it had looked darned sexy on him, too.

The pastor began to speak, and she tried to concentrate on his words so she would forget Stone. But the talk of love, commitment and devotion to family only made her think of him even more.

Once the bride and groom began repeating the vows in shaky, emotion-laden voices, she had to stop listening for her own peace of mind. In her heart, she wished them all the happiness life could give them, but hearing the words hurt too much right now.

Before she knew it the guests broke into a round of applause. Looking to the front of the church, she saw the happy couple, hand in hand, starting the walk down the aisle together.

Her grandmother patted her hand. "Wasn't that beautiful, Patty?" she said in a teary voice.

"Yes, Grandma."

Dorothy dug through her purse and pulled out a hankie. "I just love weddings. I'll cry even more at yours, of course."

The response that came to mind was: Don't hold your breath. Instead she took her grandmother's hand and squeezed it gently.

The rest of the wedding party filed past, and then the guests started out. Patrice tried to spot Stone in the crowd, but there was a tall man right in front of her, and she couldn't see anything beyond him.

Stone stood in the church's reception hall, watching the door. He had been surprised to see Patrice at the wedding. Why had she extended her vacation?

Her changed appearance hadn't shocked him so much this time. It could be because he'd already seen her all decked out, or it might be that he was so stunned she was here.

Since being released from the hospital, he'd been busy catching up on things at the ranch with the plan to fly to Phoenix if he didn't hear from her by the end of the month. But now, here she was…or she would be soon.

Unless she tried to avoid him by giving the reception a miss and heading straight home. He knew she'd seen him in the church and that she'd been caught off guard. But he didn't think she would take the coward's way out and leave.

He knew she wasn't a coward.

One question was foremost in his mind: Why hadn't she called him? Surely she knew by now if she was pregnant or not. Maybe she was afraid to tell him, afraid he might try to take the baby from her. He could understand that. It was a legitimate fear. One he might turn into a reality. But if she wasn't expecting, why was she waiting to tell him? Surely she knew he was on pins and needles. Maybe she figured he'd assume she wasn't pregnant if she didn't call.

He had no idea what the truth was. One thing he

was positive about, though, it was time he found out.

They were both here this evening, so they might as well talk tonight.

Patrice didn't catch sight of Stone again, until they entered the reception hall.

He must have been watching for them, since he headed in their direction immediately. Patrice wasn't sure, but he seemed to be favoring his right leg.

"Stone," Dorothy greeted him as he arrived.

He nodded. "Evenin', ladies."

"Hello, Stone," Patrice said.

"I'm surprised to see you, Patrice. I'd figured you would have left for Arizona ages ago."

Grandma's face lit up and Patrice's heart dropped to her shoes. "Oh, then you don't know? Patty has moved to Clancy."

One dark brow raised in question. "Really? I had no idea."

There was a commotion at the door. Finished with the posed photos, the bridal party entered the reception hall and began the receiving line.

"Grandma, shouldn't we get in line to congratulate the bride and groom?"

"Yes, of course. Stone, would you join us?" Dorothy asked.

Patrice cringed inside. She didn't need this. But

the damage had already been done. Stone accepted the offer and the three of them went to the end of the line.

She went through the motions of saying hello and talking to the other guests in line. But all the time her attention was focused on Stone being so close and the baby growing within her.

He didn't say anything that gave any hint of what had passed between them. But his presence by her side was disturbing. She felt paranoid, wondering who might know about the time they'd spent alone in the line shack.

Sheriff Jackson, Stone's foreman, Grandma and anyone they might have told either purposely or accidentally. And would anyone who knew how long they'd been there believe that nothing sexual had gone on? It occurred to her that the doctor hadn't asked about the baby's father. Could he already know about her and Stone? Clancy was a small town....

Stone continued to stay with them as they gave their congratulations to the happy couple. And they were happy—so happy they glowed. Patrice felt a twinge of envy.

Once through the line, Grandma mingled her way to a table. Patrice and Stone followed. Several of Dorothy's friends came to talk with her.

Stone took the opportunity to scoot his chair closer to Patrice. "So, you've moved to Clancy?"

"I, um, since I had to start from scratch again, I decided that I might as well do it here so I could be closer to Grandma."

He nodded. "What is it that you do exactly?"

"I had a bookkeeping service in Phoenix."

He settled more comfortably in his chair, but his gaze was intent and watchful. "Planning on starting one here?"

"I haven't decided. At the moment I'm working at the yarn and hobby shop and doing their books."

"You never did tell me how you lost your job or your fiancé. Although you implied there was a connection between the two."

She shrugged. "Oh, there's a connection, all right. But it's embarrassing." Linking her hands together in her lap, she continued, "Neil wiped out my bank accounts and skipped town."

"Did he work for you?"

"No, I met him at a friend's birthday party. We dated several months, then got engaged. One night while I was working late, he stopped by the office with dinner. I had my computer on, and I'd already gone through all the password checks so everything was accessible."

"I don't know much about computers."

"They don't have to be set up with passwords, but I had mine secured to protect the business and my clients. After dinner that night, Neil lulled me to sleep with a foot rub and cleaned out all the

accounts. Money from the business and some be-
longing to clients.''

''Any chance of catching him?''

''The police weren't optimistic. Apparently he's
been at this kind of thing for a number of years in
several states. Besides, by the time they find him,
he'll probably already have spent my money.''

''Are the clients suing you?''

''Fortunately, I had enough in other accounts he
didn't find to cover the clients' losses. But not
enough to keep myself in business.''

''Was the relationship in trouble before he did
this?''

She laughed. ''Obviously if his whole purpose
was to rob me blind, the relationship was in trouble
before it began.''

He ran his fingers over his chin the way he used
to do when he had a beard. Patrice's fingers itched
to do the same.

''Did you sense anything?'' he asked.

''No.'' She looked down. ''Which makes the
whole thing even worse.''

''Did you love him?''

She moved her gaze to Stone. What she felt in
her heart for him was so different than what she'd
felt for Neil. ''I thought I did. But maybe I was
only infatuated.''

When she almost added that perhaps her biolog-
ical clock had started ticking, she pulled herself up

short. The baby...their baby...how could she have forgotten?

She stood up. "I promised the pastor's wife I would help in the kitchen. Excuse me, please." Without waiting for an answer, she headed off.

There was plenty to do. So, keeping busy with odds and ends was easy to accomplish. The only problem was that occasionally Stone would approach her with an invitation to dance, to take a walk, or to let him help. She continued giving him lame excuse after lame excuse. He would accept each one briefly, then approach her again.

Noticing that the stack of napkins near the punch bowl was growing smaller, she headed for the pantry to get more. They were easy to find, but leaving the room was another story.

Stone stood in the doorway.

She stopped in her tracks, the napkins clutched to her chest. At first she looked at the shiny toes of his boots, then slowly raised her gaze to meet his.

"Why are you avoiding me, Patrice?"

"I'm not avoiding you. There's a lot to do."

She could see the muscles at the back of his jawline tense and release.

He didn't look happy. "And plenty of hands to share the work."

"I don't mind doing extra."

"I mind," he said.

"Why is it any of your business?"

He took a step toward her. "Because we need to talk."

"I was planning on calling you tomorrow."

He lifted one dark brow. The look in his eyes was skeptical. "Oh, of course. That's a convenient story, isn't it?"

She pulled her brows together in a frown. "Whether you believe me or not, it's the truth. And you could have called me."

It was the last thing she'd expected to say. If she could hear the hurt, the accusation in her voice, surely Stone could, too.

"I'd planned on coming to see you the day after I had dinner at your grandmother's, but I ended up in the hospital."

Shock and fear gripped her. "The hospital? What happened?"

"I slipped on a patch of ice and landed on an old knee injury."

She remembered the way he'd been favoring his right leg. "Your right knee?"

"Yes."

"How's it feeling?"

"Much better, thanks." He took another step toward her. "By the time I got home, I assumed you were already in Phoenix. I wanted to get some things done around the ranch and then I was going to head down to see you."

"In Phoenix?"

"Yes."

Why would he make the trip when her grandmother would have given him her phone number. "Why?"

"I believe we have some unfinished business."

"I...I thought everything was settled."

She bit on her bottom lip, wondering how to tell him. A church pantry was not the most conducive place to tell a man he's going to become a father. It should be a happy occasion...maybe a fireplace, or a candlelight dinner. Or like the old sitcoms where the wife sat knitting booties when the husband came home from work.

"Nothing is settled until I have an answer."

"That's not what I meant...I thought I knew the answer, but then it turns out I was wrong. And I'm planning on, er, was planning on calling you tomorrow and explaining."

"Well, I'll save you the phone call."

She remembered the napkins in her hands. "Let me put these on the table."

His eyes narrowed, but he moved out of her way. She walked swiftly to the main room and put the napkins down. When she turned, Stone was standing right behind her.

He took her elbow. "I believe this dance is mine."

Unless she pulled away and made a scene, he was going to get his way this time. She let him lead her to the dance floor. He took her into his arms and her breath caught in her throat.

The feel of him pressed against her released a flood of memories. She tilted her head back to look up at him, immediately wishing she hadn't. He was looking at her in much the same way he had before he'd kissed her the first time.

The pain building inside her was more than she could stand. Before the tears found their way to the surface she had to get away from him.

Keeping her voice low so that only he could hear, she said, "You want to know if there's a baby, of course. Well…yes, there is."

Stone came to a standstill, his hold loosening. She took advantage of the moment to move away from him and quickly head for the table. She stole a fast glance over her shoulder and was glad to see the pastor had intercepted Stone. Grandma was busy talking with friends so Patrice collected her purse and coat and headed for the parking lot.

There were a few snowflakes drifting from the sky when she got outside. Making her even more melancholy by reminding her of the cabin. By the time she drove the half mile home, the snow had picked up. The weather forecaster on the radio warned of a stormy night ahead.

When she entered the apartment, she was shivering. But she wasn't sure if it was from the cold or a delayed reaction to seeing Stone. After changing into a warm pair of sweats, she went into the kitchen and put on water for tea. She stood watching the blue flames lick the bottom of the teakettle.

Her musing was interrupted by a knock on the door.

Twelve

Patrice couldn't be sure, but she suspected it was Stone who'd knocked. Darn, she should have known he'd follow. Once again where he was concerned, she'd acted without stopping to consider the consequences.

What's happening to you, Patrice?

Her car was parked out front, so it was useless to hope he'd think she wasn't home if she didn't answer. Besides, it was inevitable that over the course of the pregnancy the two of them had to discuss the baby. They might as well get the first talk out of the way.

She turned off the stove. Pulling her shoulders

back and lifting her chin high, she walked to the door. Opening it confirmed what she'd expected. Stone was here.

His expression was grim. "Patrice, we need to talk."

"I know."

She stepped back, opening the door wider so he could enter. After taking his coat and hanging it on the coatrack, she led the way into the living room. Stone sat on the couch—well forward with his hands clasped between his open knees.

"Did you tell the truth back there? Are you really pregnant?"

"Yes."

He sat straighter and ran his splayed hands through his hair.

Patrice watched the play of emotions over his face. "I'm sorry for blurting it out the way I did. I just found out today, and I haven't gotten used to the idea myself. And I didn't expect you to be at the wedding—"

"One point at a time, please." Stone stood, tucking his hands into the pockets of his slacks. "It's hard to believe that you waited this long to find out if you were expecting. It's been well over a month."

She explained about the short period and what the doctor had said about it.

"All right, I can understand how you might have

thought you weren't pregnant. But why didn't you call me at that point?''

Patrice wrapped her arms across her chest, as though they could provide a shield. ''Last time we were together you seemed so cold and impersonal.''

''I gave you my card and told you to call me.''

''But if you'd really cared, wouldn't you have called me?''

He looked down to the floor in front of him. ''I was planning on coming over the next day to apologize for that evening.''

She remembered what he'd said at the reception. ''And then you ended up in the hospital?''

''Yes.''

''That still doesn't explain why you were so cold? You seemed different on the phone the night before.''

Stone stood and walked to her, placing his hands on her shoulders. ''I'd been looking forward to spending the evening with you. But when you opened the door, it was like seeing a total stranger.''

''Why?''

''The clothes, the hair, the makeup—during our time at the cabin you looked like another woman entirely.''

''Tonight, you look different in your suit. Especially without the beard. But I know it's you.''

''I know my reaction sounds unreasonable. I

came to that realization myself later that same night. But, unreasonable or not, when you opened the door I was knocked off track by the sight of you."

"I'm dressed up now, too. Does it bother you?"

"No. The surprise for me tonight wasn't your appearance, but your being here at all." His eyes narrowed speculatively. "If you only found out about the baby today, I take it that's not the reason you moved up here."

She wondered how he felt about her moving to Clancy, but didn't feel confident enough to ask. Not being sure she could hide her disappointment from him if his answer wasn't positive.

"No, it wasn't for the baby. I made the decision when I thought there wasn't one. Stone, I'm sorry I didn't call you when I suspected I had the answer about the baby."

He squeezed her shoulders gently. "It's just as well, isn't it? Since the answer changed."

"Still…it wasn't right for me not to tell you. But I didn't think you cared."

He brought one hand up to caress her cheek. "I care, darlin'. Believe me I care."

The question she longed to ask was whether he cared about her or the baby. Of course the answer would be the baby. While she wanted him to care for the child, she also longed for him to care for her. More than care for her—she wanted him to love her.

You might as well ask for the moon. You'd have a better chance of getting it.

Stone took her hand and led her to the couch. She sat and then he sat beside her, angling his body in her direction.

"I want to explain a few things that might help you understand where I'm coming from on this whole issue of the baby."

The serious intensity of his expression made her nervous, but she needed to hear what he had to say. "All right."

"I told you at the cabin that I've been married."

"Yes."

"Val and I had been married four years when I lost her. And we'd been a couple for five years before that."

"It must have been hard on you when she died."

He nodded. "More so because of how she died."

Patrice had wondered about this at the cabin, but hadn't felt it was her place to ask. Now that he was about to relate the details, an uneasiness settled over her. She knew Stone must have loved his wife a great deal, and suddenly she felt presumptuous thinking he could ever love her.

Stone cleared his throat. "Around our third anniversary I began to think it was time for us to start a family. Val wanted to wait a few more years, but I kept after her until she changed her mind.''

He hadn't made any mention of a child at home. Then again the subject hadn't come up. Her attention focused on Stone once more when he began to speak.

''It took us six months to get pregnant. Val was seven months along when it came time for spring roundup. She'd been doing fine, so it never crossed my mind to leave someone at the house with her or check in during the day.''

He closed his eyes tightly, deep furrows lined his brow.

Patrice rested her hand over his. ''If you'd rather not tell me, I'll understand.''

Stone met her gaze. ''I think you should know.''

She did feel a need to know, but she felt that his need to tell was even greater. ''All right.''

''We'll never know exactly what happened, but the conclusions were that she had a miscarriage, then continued to hemorrhage. I have no idea why she didn't call the doctor. The phone was on the nightstand beside the bed.''

''I'm so sorry, Stone.''

''Whether you like it or not, because of our baby, my life and yours are going to be connected from here on out.''

In her heart she knew he was right—the child

would always be a link between them. "I suppose in some respects it's inevitable."

He glanced toward her stomach. "It is. That's why I think you need to know how much this child means to me."

She braced herself for a barrage of reasons why he should get custody of their baby.

Instead he said, "Don't get me wrong. No matter what the past held, I would have loved this baby. But because of the way things happened, this child means even more to me. It's a chance I thought I'd never have again."

Demands would have been easier for her to refuse, easier to ignore and block out of her heart than his sorrow. What she wanted to do was tell him she loved him, ask him to take both the baby *and* her, let them fill his life.

She didn't know if ultimately she could make him happy, but she did know that with all her heart and soul she wanted to try.

"Stone, you're young—you have many years left to have more children."

"But truthfully, I don't know if I could ever have made the choice to try again. Val's gone, and I'll always wonder if I hadn't convinced her to have a baby then, whether she would still be here."

She could feel the depths of his emotions. "You're carrying a hefty burden of guilt tangled with your sadness."

"Yes, I guess I am. I may always. But all that is only incidental to what we're facing now. I just wanted you to know my side of things."

"Thank you for explaining."

He took one of her hands in his. "Something special happened between us at the cabin. I'm not sure what. I might have been on the way to falling in love with you."

The word love was there. But the words "might have been" cast a shadow over any joy she could have felt. She had no idea what to say.

Luckily Stone continued, "With the baby on the way, my first instinct is to offer marriage. Part of me wants to grab this second chance for happiness, but part of me worries that history might repeat itself if I try again."

Despite her disappointment, she did follow his reasoning. "I understand your fear."

She understood, but that didn't stop the hurt his rejection caused. It was just as well that he didn't offer marriage, though. Patrice had no wish for her and her baby to simply be substitutes for those he'd lost.

"I hope you can also understand when I ask for some time to think through things."

"I could use some time, too. After all, I just got the news today myself."

"Of course. I should have realized." He let go

of her hand and stood. "I'd better be heading home."

She knew it was the best answer, but still what she really wanted was to be swept into his arms and carried off to bed. What she really needed was to lose herself in his kisses, in his touch. To relive the exquisite pleasure that had brought their child into being.

It wasn't likely to happen while Stone was grieving for his first wife and their baby.

Stone drove home half-dazed. He was going to be a father.

Patrice had looked so vulnerable when she'd opened the door of her apartment, he'd had a strong urge to sweep her into his arms and hold her close. This whole thing was hard on him, and he knew it had to be hard on her, too.

It also bothered him that before he knew about the baby, he'd been pleased to hear she'd moved to Clancy. He wondered why it made a difference to him. Was it just a matter of great sex? Was that what he wanted their future to hold?

Then again, maybe his pleasure in knowing she'd moved closer was because he wanted the chance to build more to their relationship.

Could he be falling in love with her?

The first moment he'd laid eyes on Val, he'd fallen deeply in love. Nothing that dramatic had happened with Patrice. He'd been emotionally indifferent to her at first—although he'd acknowledged she was attractive. She was nothing more than a damsel in distress he was trying to rescue. But then they'd started getting to know each other.

So what was it he was feeling now—friendship, lust or could it be love? If it was love, then who was he in love with? The woman as she appeared now or the woman from the cabin. Or had the woman at the cabin only been someone he'd created in his mind?

Then again, maybe what he felt was only the deep, desperate yearning to have true love in his life again.

Val's loss had hit him hard, frozen his heart, numbed him…were these strange feelings the first tingles of defrosting? Had he mistaken the beginning signs of life for possible signs of love?

Regardless of his feelings for Patrice, there was no doubt in his mind that he loved their child. And he loved it as much as he'd loved the baby Val had been carrying.

Why did he feel the same about the babies, when what he felt for Patrice was different than what he'd felt for his first wife? That was a big part of his uncertainty about whether what he felt for Patrice was really love.

Besides, what he felt wasn't all that mattered. She hadn't said anything about loving him either.

* * *

Patrice was still tired when she woke the next morning. So although she didn't remember having any bad dreams, she knew she hadn't slept peacefully.

She needed to get her vitamin prescription filled. Yesterday she'd been too stunned by the news that she hadn't thought to do it on her way home. There was plenty of time to take care of it before heading to Grandma's.

Last night's storm hadn't left nearly as much snow as the radio had estimated. She decided to walk, since the pharmacy was only half a block down Main Street.

Once there, she turned in her prescription and headed to the greeting cards to choose one for her mother's birthday. The bell over the door rang, signaling another customer had entered the store.

Patrice glanced up. Her breath caught in her throat when she spotted Stone. Hoping he didn't see her was futile since he headed directly for her.

"Good mornin'," he said.

"Hello, Stone." She kept her tone cool and polite in keeping with his casual greeting. Although something more intimate, more befitting expectant parents would have felt so good. It broke her heart to think that, although they'd conceived a child together, such a wide chasm separated them.

He glanced at the card she was holding. "Your mother having a birthday?"

"In a few weeks."

"That's nice."

"Stone," the pharmacist called out. "I've got your refill ready."

Stone waved to the man. "Be there in a minute."

"Aren't you feeling well?" Patrice asked.

"Just needed some more painkillers for the knee. I've been spending too much time on it."

"You should take it easier."

He shrugged, then adjusted his hat. "Do you have plans for the rest of the day?"

"Grandma and I are planning to clean out her attic."

"I was hoping we could go somewhere to talk."

She was glad she already had plans. Not at all sure that she was ready to talk to him about the baby again. "I'm not sure how long it will take us."

"Please?"

There was a depth of emotion in his voice that made it impossible for her to refuse. "I'm sure Grandma won't mind if we postpone."

"Would you like to come out to my place?"

She'd assumed they would go to her apartment or to the local coffee shop, but she was curious to see his ranch. "All right. Let me call Grandma and then get my truck."

"No need. I'll drive."

"But then you'll have to bring me back later to-day."

"I don't mind. The roads are icy, and I'd rather you rode with me."

"I've been learning."

"I'm sure you have. Let me grab my prescription." He turned and headed to the pickup window.

She followed. "I have one, too."

He looked at her, one brow raised in question. "Are you all right?"

"It's for prenatal vitamins."

He nodded. "Good."

When they reached the counter, he let her go first. She paid for her prescription and the card. "I'll call from the pay phone out front."

"I'll meet you there."

Grandma was understanding about moving their plans to another day, especially when she heard the reason.

Patrice wanted to squelch any hopes for match-making that Dorothy might be conjuring up, but knew the task would be useless once word was out about the baby.

As she hung up the phone, Stone walked out the door, heading toward her. "Ready to go?"

"Yes. Grandma said to tell you hello."

"Return the message for me, all right?"

"Sure."

He gestured toward his pickup. "This way."

When they reached the truck, he opened the passenger door for her. She hopped in. He closed the door behind her.

Why are you doing this, Patrice? You should be staying as far away from him as possible until you know he's not going to try to steal your baby.

A brief moment of panic struck as she waited for him to circle the pickup and get in on his side. It settled once he was seated and the engine roared to life.

On the drive to the ranch, Patrice noticed a few snowflakes starting to fall. The farther they got from town the more of them there were. "I thought the forecast said the snow would end early this morning."

"It did, but occasionally the experts are wrong. From the color of the clouds, I'd say we're in for quite a bit of the white stuff."

"Maybe we should just talk at my place."

He glanced her way, flashing one of his killer smiles. "Why? If we get stranded, we'll have all the modern conveniences this time. The ranch even has indoor plumbing."

Despite her instincts, which warned her not to let him lull her into complacency with his charm, she smiled back at him. "I'm glad to hear that."

Stone pointed out the fence post that marked the beginning of the Baron Garrett Cattle Company land. She was surprised to hear that it stretched before them on both sides of the highway.

There were brief spouts of small talk along the way, but for the most part they were silent. Patrice would occasionally glance toward him, tracing the lines of his profile with her gaze. Despite her misgivings about the problems he might give her by trying to take the baby, it felt good to be with him. She wanted so much to slip across the bench seat and rest her head on his shoulder, put her hand on the denim covering his thigh.

Stone flipped on his left-turn signal. Once off the highway, he drove over a cattle crossing and continued down a well-maintained road, passing under an archway with a large version of the ranch's nested G and C brand displayed overhead.

The road curved and headed upward into a series of rolling hills nestled at the bottom of tall mountains. Beyond the first lay a valley, larger than she would have expected. Scattered around were a number of buildings of various sizes and fenced-off areas. Sitting well back and up the closest slope was a large white Victorian-style house. Swirling snowflakes enhanced, rather than obscured the view.

Stone stopped the truck on the crest of the hill entering the valley. "What do you think?"

"It's much bigger than I expected. And more modern looking. Other than the house."

"Were you expecting an old weatherworn red barn and a few corrals?"

She smiled. "It sounds silly when you put it that way. But, yes, that's what I was expecting."

He laughed. "Don't feel bad, that's what most people expect when they hear cattle ranch. The red barn, lots of wide-open spaces and cowboys."

"Two out of three isn't bad," she said.

He laughed again, then faced forward and put the truck into gear. Before entering the work area, there was a turnoff that led them to the house. Stone drove into the open garage at the back.

They got out of the truck and walked across the yard. The rear of the house was as beautiful as the front. With wide wraparound porches and gingerbread trim.

"What a lovely house," she said.

"The baron built it for his bride as a wedding gift."

"How romantic."

"According to family legend he was quite the charmer."

Not unlike his great-great-grandson, Patrice thought, but didn't dare say out loud.

Stone led the way up the stairs, but instead of going in the back door, he took the porch around to the front. Opening the carved wooden door, he motioned her past him.

The inside of the house continued quaint charm

and detailed craftsmanship. From what she could glimpse of the rooms off the entryway, some of the furniture looked as though it might have originally been the baron's as well.

It was in good shape, dust free and polished to a high gloss. She doubted Stone took the time for that. He must have a housekeeper.

He showed her the ground floor, including his office with a painting of the baron over the fireplace. The formidable-looking ancestor bore a striking resemblance to Stone, even though his hair was blond.

They also lingered awhile in the den where Stone's Labrador retriever, Elwood, was sprawled in front of the fireplace, even though the fire wasn't lit. Once they finished the tour, Stone took her back to the living room.

He gestured to the couch. "Have a seat."

"Thanks." She sat at one end, sinking into the soft leather.

She wondered why he didn't offer to show her upstairs. But it was just as well; the bedrooms were probably up there, including Stone's. She would like to see it, but knew if she did visions of him in it would haunt her in the dark hours of the night.

"Would you like something to drink?" Stone asked.

"Maybe later."

He sat toward the middle of the sofa, angled in

her direction. They both began speaking at once, then laughed.

"Ladies first," he said.

"I was only going to compliment you on the inside of the house."

"Thanks. I've dug out a lot of the original furniture from the attic and had it refinished."

She glanced around the room. "It's nice." Her gaze moved to Stone and her breath caught in her throat at the look in his eyes. The fire and spark she'd seen at the cabin was there again.

"Stone?" His name was a question and a sigh.

He crossed the distance between them, until there were only a few inches separating them. Holding her gaze with his, he ran one finger along her cheek and under her chin, tilting her face up to him. Leaning forward he moved his mouth over hers in a gentle kiss.

Patrice lifted her hands to rest on the hard wall of his chest. Her heart skipped a beat and her spirits soared. The long days and weeks between now and their time at the cabin telescoped into seconds at the feel, taste and scent of him.

And now there was only the unhampered scent of him. No lingering residual tang of wood smoke.

She let the familiar sensations flood her, blocking out everything but the man holding her in his arms. It felt as right as it always had. And the strong desire to move well beyond kisses began to torment her.

Putting all the longing in her heart and body into the act, she kissed him back. After long passion-filled moments, Stone moved his lips from hers and gathered her tightly against him.

"I love you, Patrice. Although it's taken me awhile to realize it for what it is." His voice was a husky whisper next to her ear. His breath warm against her skin.

She pulled back slightly so she could look at him. The sincerity she saw in his blue eyes both stunned and thrilled her. "I love you, too."

He looked surprised. "How long have you known?"

"I knew while we were at the cabin."

"You never said anything."

"It didn't seem like something you'd be interested in hearing. And I didn't want to jeopardize what we had."

He moved his hands in soothing circles over her back. "It took me a long time to recognize what I was feeling. I'm sorry."

"Don't be sorry. I'm sure there's a good reason."

"Not what I consider a good reason, but the only one I have." He settled against the back of the couch, adjusting her so she rested comfortably in his arms. "Although I didn't realize it, in the past few years I've only been going through the motions of living. My heart and emotions have been frozen since I lost Val.''

"You must have loved her very much."

"I did. And in a way I always will. But my heart was shut off from everything else in life until, in a cabin in the snow, a sassy redhead brought me in from the cold, melting the ice around my heart with her warmth."

She could feel the heat of a blush stain her cheeks. "I don't know what to say."

"Well...since you've already said, I love you. How about saying that you'll marry me?"

"Marry you?"

He chuckled. "Isn't that what two people do when they love each other?"

She caught her bottom lip between her teeth. "I guess. All of this has caught me by surprise."

"That's what you did to me, too. And although it took me longer than it should have to realize it, I can't think of anything I'd like better than having you living here with me every day like you did at the cabin."

The thought sounded wonderful to her, too. But something had changed; there was an added factor that hadn't been there in the cabin. "Stone, we won't be alone long. The baby," she reminded him.

He smiled. "No problem. I'm going to love having another sassy redhead in my life."

One last niggling doubt troubled her. "If there wasn't a baby...would you still be asking me to marry you?"

He sighed. "I wish you trusted me enough not to have to ask. But between your ex and my behavior lately, I know that's a lot to ask for. I'll just have to prove to you that I love you with all my heart. And yes, even without the baby I'd want to marry you."

She slipped her arms around him, pulling him close. "Yes, my love. Yes, I'll marry you. There's nothing I want more."

"Good."

Over his shoulder, Patrice glanced out the window. "The snow is really coming down now."

Stone turned to look, then turned his gaze back to her. "I guess we'll be snowed in for the night."

She raised one brow in question. "How often does getting snowed in happen around here?"

"Not nearly enough for me...even with a whole future full of snowstorms together."

Epilogue

Patrice finished diapering her daughter, Gwen, closed up the sleeper and lifted her into her arms. She walked to the window, pulled back the ruffled pink curtains decorated with pictures of fluffy, pink teddy bears and looked out. A flash of movement to the right caught her attention. Stone was on horseback, heading for the barn.

"Well, sweetpea, it looks like you'll get to see Daddy before bedtime, after all."

Gwen cooed and smiled, waving chubby fists in the air.

Patrice kissed her nose and laughed. "Too cute. Just a little chip off the old block."

Actually a chip off both blocks—the baby had her red hair, but her father's blue eyes.

Patrice held the baby close, inhaling the sweet scents of baby shampoo and powder. "What do you think? Are you ready to go downstairs?"

Gwen bounced up and down as if she were sitting on a spring.

"I take it that's a yes."

Patrice headed for the kitchen. She put a bottle of formula in a pan of water to heat. While waiting she gazed out the window again, watching for Stone to come out of the barn. It wasn't long before she saw him striding up the hill to the house, his hands tucked deep into the pockets of his jacket. Elwood bounded along beside him.

They came in through the service porch. Elwood padded straight in and curled up in front of the stove. Stone stopped to leave his coat, hat and boots in the porch before continuing into the kitchen.

Smiling, he kissed Patrice on the cheek before taking Gwen from her. She looked tiny in her daddy's arms. "Hey, little darlin'. Have you been a good girl today?"

"Tell Daddy that you're always a good girl."

Stone laughed.

"Well...most of the time," Patrice amended.

He winked at his wife. "Just like her mommy."

Patrice checked the bottle. The temperature was perfect.

"Is that ready?" Stone asked.

"Yes."

"I'll take her up and put her to bed."

"All right. I'll put the finishing touches on dinner."

Stone took the bottle, kissed his wife again and left the room babbling nonsense to Gwen.

Once dinner was on the table, Patrice stood in front of the sink and looked out the window. The green grass was mostly faded to pale gold. And the deciduous trees had passed through their fall colors and lost their leaves.

Stone slipped his arms around her from behind, startling her. He placed a soft kiss on the back of her neck.

"It looks cold out there," she said, leaning back against him and wrapping her arms over his.

"It is. Winter's definitely on the way. Are you ready for cold weather again? Maybe some snow or a blizzard?"

"Let the winter begin." She glanced at the ceiling. "I know someplace where it's always warm."

He placed one hand on each of her hips and took another step forward, pressing tightly. "Hmm...and I'll bet I can help you make it even warmer...hot even."

She tilted her head back and looked up at him. "Dinner's ready."

"It can be warmed up later. That's what microwaves are for."

She smiled. "You don't mind having dinner reheated?"

He traced one finger down her nose and across her lips. "Not at all. And if I remember correctly, this won't be the first time."

"Not even the first time this week."

"You're most likely right, darlin'." He swept her into his arms. "Let's get naked and share a little body heat, Mrs. Garrett."

* * * * *

▼™ SILHOUETTE
DESIRE®

AVAILABLE FROM 19TH NOVEMBER 1999

The Perfect Fit Cait London

A TallChief Man of the Month

Nick Palladin refuses to marry Silver Tallchief just for the sake of a
business deal, but when she moves into his home and sends his
hormones haywire, suddenly he can't wait!

The Sheriff and the Impostor Bride Elizabeth Bevarly

Follow That Baby

Her pregnant twin was missing! Strapping sheriff Riley Hunter was
convinced she was the mum-to-be. Should she admit the truth?

His Ultimate Temptation Susan Crosby

An independent woman and an overprotective man, they'd loved but
parted as 'just friends'. Now trapped together their primitive desires are
irresistible…

Just a Little Bit Married? Eileen Wilks

Dark, brooding Raz Rasmussin had been hired to protect Sara Grace, so
they were posing as newlyweds, but they began to take the honeymoon
too seriously!

The Millionaire's Christmas Wish Shawna Delacorte

Millionaire Chance Fowler kissed a pretty stranger to dodge the press who
followed him. But then he couldn't forget her, so he had to find her…

Marriage, Outlaw Style Cindy Gerard

Outlaw Hearts

Waking up next to Clay James was absolutely crazy, even if he was
gorgeous and had come to her rescue. Suddenly, Maddie Brannigan was
in trouble—the 6lb 12oz kind!

FREE!

4 Books
and a surprise gift!

We would like to take this opportunity to thank you for reading this Silhouette® book by offering you the chance to take FOUR more specially selected titles from the Desire™ series absolutely FREE! We're also making this offer to introduce you to the benefits of the Reader Service™—

★ FREE home delivery
★ FREE gifts and competitions
★ FREE monthly Newsletter
★ Books available before they're in the shops
★ Exclusive Reader Service discounts

Accepting these FREE books and gift places you under no obligation to buy; you may cancel at any time, even after receiving your free shipment. Simply complete your details below and return the entire page to the address below. *You don't even need a stamp!*

YES! Please send me 4 free Desire books and a surprise gift. I understand that unless you hear from me, I will receive 6 superb new titles every month for just £2.70 each, postage and packing free. I am under no obligation to purchase any books and may cancel my subscription at any time. The free books and gift will be mine to keep in any case.

D9EB

Ms/Mrs/Miss/Mr ....Initials ....
BLOCK CAPITALS PLEASE

Surname ....

Address ....

....

....Postcode ....

Send this whole page to:
UK: The Reader Service, FREEPOST CN81, Croydon, CR9 3WZ
EIRE: The Reader Service, PO Box 4546, Kilcock, County Kildare (stamp required)